Halo in Brass

Dennis McMillan Publications Paperbacks

The Fredric Brown Pulp Detective Series

Homicide Sanitarium
Before She Kills
Thirty Corpses Every Thursday
The Freak Show Murders
Pardon My Ghoulish Laughter

The Classic Hard-Boiled Series

Blue Murder by Robert Leslie Bellem
42 Days for Murder by Roger Torrey
Halo in Brass by Howard Browne
The Vice Czar Murders
by Robert Leslie Bellem & Cleve F. Adams
Half-Past Mortem by Robert Leslie Bellem

The Modern Hard-Boiled Series

The Blind Pig by Jon A. Jackson
The Taste of Ashes by Howard Browne
Kiss Your Ass Goodbye by Charles Willeford
Understudy for Death by Charles Willeford

Classic Erotica

The Ups & Downs of Life
by Capt. Edward Sellon

Literature

The Given Day by Robert van Gulik
Whores by James Crumley

Mohonk Mysteries by Don & Abby Westlake

Transylvania Station
High Jinx

Halo in Brass

Howard Browne

1988

This book was originally printed in hardcover by
Bobbs-Merrill in 1949.

Cover by Joe Servello

Published September 1988

Dennis McMillan Publications
Missoula, Monatana
Distributed by
Creative Arts Book Company
833 Bancroft Way
Berkeley, California 94710

Foreword

In 1946, Bobbs-Merrill brought out the first Paul Pine novel, *Halo in Blood.* It did well with both reviewers and readers—so well, in fact, that I developed delusions of grandeur, quit my job as magazine editor, and set out to seek fame and fortune as a free-lance writer.

And damned near starved to death.

Bobbs-Merrill had given me a contract and a thousand-dollar advance (big money in '47) on the next book, but only if I agreed to get it to them in time for their Spring 1948, list. By the time I'd moved my family from Chicago to Burbank, California, bought a home there and settled in, I had five—count 'em, five—weeks to write a complete novel from scratch. Even worse, I hadn't the slightest inkling of a plot to start with.

The novel turned out to be *Halo for Satan* and I did meet the deadline. Meeting it put a sprinkling of gray in the plentiful supply of hair I had at the time, came close to ending my marriage, and left me with a bad case of writer's block that took months to break.

But I did get something else out of the experience. A device—a gimmick if you will. In short: turn out mystery novels in which the least likely suspect is *not* the killer, but somebody *impossible* to suspect!

While I tried to bring off such a device in *Halo in Brass,* it is not one I'd use in today's market. It is built around lesbianism and reflects the attitude toward homosexuality that was prevalent in and before 1949—an attitude shared by Pine and the circles he moved in. And admittedly shared, at the time, by the author as well; otherwise he would not—and could not—have written the book.

However, aside from that, I believe *Halo in Brass* is as good a novel as I was able to write back then. Whether it holds up forty years later is something I must leave for the reader to decide.

Howard Browne
Carlsbad, California
March, 1988

FOR MY EDITOR

HARRISON PLATT

. . . PATIENCE, CAJOLERY, AND THE KNOUT

CHAPTER 1

ALMOST the first thing Mrs. Fremont said after I was seated on the edge of her lounge chair was that Laura had always been a good girl. She tried to sound aggressive about it, in case I had picked up the wrong idea somewhere along the line and needed to be straightened out.

"Nothing else than just being thoughtless, Mr. Pine. Away from home and busy with her work and new friends and all. Youngsters kind of take their folks for granted sometimes."

"So I've heard," I said.

"Course I'm a mite surprised Laura's not more thoughtful. Pa and I done our level best to give her a good Christian raising and she's always been a credit to us. But she was always kind of . . . well, headstrong I guess you'd call it."

"High-spirited," I suggested.

We were sitting in a small airless parlor and beaming across at each other. They were Mr. and Mrs. Charles J. Fremont, both in their sixties, frail-bodied, skin filled with thin shallow wrinkles and yellowing a little like the linen in an old maid's hope chest. Both were in their Sunday best, both sincere and troubled and too proud to let a stranger see how deeply they were troubled.

They sat side by side on a rust-colored mohair sofa with carved trimming in dark walnut to match the rest of the overstuffed, massive-legged pieces jammed into the small square room. It was a room that had become hostile and aloof from not having visitors come into it more often. The local pastor would make the grade once in a while, but hardly anyone else.

A nine-by-twelve Wilton rug with a border of angry-pink roses covered most of the varnished oak floor, looking as stiffly glazed as a section of new linoleum. Above the couch a pastoral print direct from a mail-order house covered an oblong segment of pale-tan wallpaper featuring a green climbing vine. In one corner the shelves of a whatnot stand were crowded with bits of ivory and glass and porcelain that gleamed dully in the half-light. Old-fashioned green shades were drawn behind russet draperies to shut out some of the solid dry heat of a prairie afternoon.

Mrs. Fremont was doing the talking. She was one of those small birdlike females who are active in church socials and the local chapter of the Eastern Star, and who work up quite a reputation for strawberry preserves. She would go into her eighties and die with patient resignation, knowing in advance that the wings would fit and the harp would be in tune.

"Then, too," she went on, her words sturdy with their Midwestern twang, "Laura always was so pretty." She sighed gently and fumbled at the heavy gold wedding band on the proper finger. "Sometimes being pretty can kind of turn a girl's head. Don't you think so, Mr. Pine?"

I bit back a yawn and rolled my thumbs and said she was certainly right about that. Any minute now she'd run down on the small talk and we could get around to the problem at hand.

"Clara," Charles Fremont said unexpectedly, "this gentleman's likely in a hurry. Tell him what we got to say."

It surprised me into staring at him. Up till now his share in the conversation had been held down to breathing and knuckle popping. He was a tall gangling man who wore a necktie as though it were a hangman's noose and who would never be really at ease without a plow to lean on.

His was the correct idea, but it was wasted on Clara Fremont. Her thin colorless lips got even thinner. "Now, Pa. We're just visiting. We don't want Mr. Pine to think we're not neighborly." She unlimbered a bright quick smile, showing chalk-white teeth the dentist had probably overcharged her for. "It was real nice of you to come all the way to Lincoln this way, Mr. Pine."

"I needed a few days off," I said. "And Nebraska is just far enough from Chicago to make it a nice drive."

She believed me, although that hardly seemed possible.

"Well, I certainly do hope you can find Laura for us without going to much trouble. Not only because of the money, I mean. Although I must say five dollars a day does sound real reasonable. Pa and I both thought it would cost a mint to hire a detective."

"I take on more than one case at a time," I said gravely. "That way it works out fine."

"Well, I must say Pa and I are real grateful for what you're doing. We know Laura's a grown-up girl now and got her own life to lead. But . . . Pa and me, we worry . . . In a big city like Chicago that way. If she'd only write . . . even a post card. Almost a year since we heard . . . "

Her voice began to fall apart and two tears spilled over and started a crooked path through the thin layer of rice powder on her wrinkled cheeks. The old man squirmed a little and popped another knuckle and looked at the wall over my head.

It was all in a day's work. "Usually," I said, "I do pretty well at finding people. But I'll have to know some things to start."

Mrs. Fremont ducked her head long enough to dig a small square of cambric from the bosom of her shirtwaist and pat her eyes. When she looked up again her faded blue eyes had a new brightness and her voice was up off the canvas. "We'll tell you anything we can, Mr. Pine."

I fished a cigarette from behind the display handkerchief in my breast pocket and lighted it. Mrs. Fremont looked almost shocked at having tobacco burning in her parlor, but I figured being a private detective at five dollars a day should at least entitle me to smoke on the job. I peered around for an ash tray, ready to give odds I wouldn't find one. Mrs. Fremont got up and found a small white saucer with a state seal printed in the bowl part and SOUVENIR OF DENVER, COLORADO in blue letters across the bottom. I thanked her and put it down on the starched lace antimacassar covering the arm of my lounge chair and dropped the used match in it. No match ever looked lonelier.

They were watching me, waiting for the big city detective to get out his bottle of fingerprint powder and enlarging glass. I blew smoke through my nose as a substitute for something startling and said, "Exactly how long ago did Laura go to Chicago?"

"Almost two years, Mr. Pine."

"Any certain type of work she expected to get into?"

"An office secretary. She was good at typewriting and shorthand and bookkeeping."

"Uh-hunh. She go to college?"

"Two years of business college. We couldn't afford it to be the university here in Lincoln. She went through high school with the highest grades in all her classes. Just wonderful in play acting, too. The loveliest speaking voice you can imagine."

"I see. Laura have a lot of friends?"

"Well, I should say so! House was always just full of girls. Hardly a night one of them didn't stay over."

"You checked with any of them, Mrs. Fremont? They might be getting mail from her."

It was a new idea to her and she frowned over it before slowly shaking her head. "She wouldn't be writing to them. Most all her friends got married and Laura stopped seeing them. Married folks don't mix much with the single ones. You know how that is."

"I'm afraid not, Mrs. Fremont."

For some obscure reason the remark interested her. "Don't tell me a nice-looking young man like you's not married."

"No," I said. "This dent in my nose came from high-school football."

It wasn't funny, it wasn't even bright, but it was broad enough for almost anyone to understand. Yet it went past the Fremonts like a rifle bullet. Nothing changed in the old man's labored study of the wall, while his wife beamed at me in a politely baffled way.

I dropped cigarette ash in the souvenir saucer and said gently, "What about your daughter's boy friends? Any of them waiting for her to get tired of the big city and come home to a church wedding?"

" . . . No."

A reply from her that short made me blink. I hadn't missed the brief hesitation ahead of it, either. This might be an angle worth digging into. I got out my pick and shovel and went to work.

"That sounds a little unusual, Mrs. Fremont. I mean, a beautiful, talented girl like Laura?"

"She didn't have no time for boys." Her voice had taken on a falsely bright quality. "Laura was bound and determined she was going to be a business girl. I guess studying and boys don't work out together."

"I see." I saw everything—and nothing. "Couldn't she have found office work here in Lincoln? Seems like a sizable town. Couldn't it be she *was* interested in some young man, Mrs. Fremont? Maybe it didn't work out for some reason she didn't tell you about. That might explain why she went to Chicago."

She was shaking her head before I had finished. "That wouldn't be it at all," she said stiffly. "Ever since high school Laura wanted to go to some place like Chicago or New York. She always would say this town wasn't big enough—that everybody knew your business."

That last part made no particular sense as far as I could tell. The picture I was getting of Laura Fremont had nothing in it the neighbors could do much with even in a smaller town. I blew more smoke through the same nose, crossed my legs the other way and rubbed my hand thoughtfully around on my kneecap.

"You say it's been two years since she went to Chicago?" I asked.

"Yes, sir."

"She stopped writing when?"

"This last January."

I ticked the months between off on my fingers. "Little over eight months then?"

"Yes, sir."

"Up to then you heard from her regularly?"

"Yes, sir."

"You still have those letters?"

"Yes, sir."

"Before I go, I'd like to look them over. And I'll need a picture. The latest one you can find."

She had started to get up, but my last few words dropped her back onto the couch again as if all the strength had suddenly run out of her. Her mouth came open a little and she made a weak kind of mewing noise that finally got loud enough to be words. "There . . . I'm . . . There isn't any . . . any picture."

I blinked at her. The silence was as heavy as the bottom of a glacier and getting heavier. Even the old man had managed to get his eyes off the wall and was staring at her. I got rid of my cigarette, took out my handkerchief and mopped the back of my neck and put it away again. What at first had seemed one of those simple little cases, no headaches and no night work, was beginning to take on distorted lines. The kind of lines that had to be followed but could lead to unexpected and uncomfortable situations.

This business of no pictures, for instance. That wasn't right. Everybody has his picture taken at one time or another. Especially a girl, unless she looks like the Witch of Endor. If not a studio portrait then at least a picnic snapshot or one having fun at the carnival.

I said slowly, "Why not, Mrs. Fremont? Was your daughter camera shy?"

The silence had lasted long enough for her to pick up the pieces. "We had lots of pictures of her," she said in a faraway voice. "Only . . . "

"Only what, Mrs. Fremont?"

"She took them away. All of them. I didn't know until one day I was looking through the albums. I can't understand why she'd take them—all of them—that way."

Neither could I. But I didn't say so. Saying so would only have dimmed the trust in me shining out of those faded blue eyes. Instead I said, "If there isn't, there isn't. Maybe if you'd describe her it would do as well. Height, weight, color of hair and eyes."

She took a stab at it. Leaving out the glowing adjectives, Laura Fremont was about five-feet-eight—taller than I expected, judging from her parents—light-brown hair, blue eyes, a hundred and forty pounds. Evidently a nice solid hunk of girl, corn-fed and full of vitality.

I finished making notes on the back of an envelope and Mrs. Fremont went off somewhere and unearthed a thin packet of letters. The red ribbon around them in a double loop had a glazed look and GILLEN'S CANDIES printed on it in white letters that were beginning to flake off. The envelopes bore Chicago post-office cancellations over a period of thirteen months, the last one dated the middle of January of the present year. Number one showed a return address: a YWCA on North Dearborn Street, an underhand toss from Chicago's Loop. The remaining seven gave 1682 North LaSalle Street as her residence.

Very quickly I went through the enclosures looking for information. For what I wanted, they were a waste of time. No names or addresses of friends, no employer or company identified by name. Nothing but flowery descriptions of the city and the titles of movies she'd seen and full details on how she cured a couple of bad colds. Guarded letters, carefully vague, deliberately worded to say nothing and to say it at length. Nothing but the two return addresses. Those I could have had by calling the Fremonts long distance.

I put the addresses down on the same envelope with Laura's dimensions and handed back the letters. "That's fine," I said with as much heartiness as I could dredge up. "A couple more questions and I'll be on my way."

The old lady seemed to sense my disappointment. "Anything at all, Mr. Pine," she quavered.

"Did your daughter have a job already lined up in Chicago, or did she go at it cold?"

"She just up and went," Mrs. Fremont said. "She was awful confident, Laura was. She was that way all her life, almost. She'd up and look people right in the eye and go straight ahead. Nothing fluttery about her, I tell you!"

I couldn't tell whether she was proud or regretful. I said, "Any of her Lincoln friends ever move to Chicago? People she might look up when she got there for old time's sake?"

She thought about it before shaking her head no. "Not that I know about, Mr. Pine. You think of any, Pa?"

He pried his gaze off the wall and clawed at his cheek while turning the question over in his slow mind. "Well now, there was that Rehak girl, Clara. Didn't she go to Chicago awhile back?"

Two spots of color began to glow in Clara Fremont's aged cheeks. She glared at him. "You know how that girl turned out, Charles. Laura wouldn't go near her!"

It dried him up in a hurry, but there could be something in what he had said for me to get my teeth into. I said, "Laura's letters weren't much help. I'm going to need any lead I can get. Tell me about this Rehak girl. Parents still in Lincoln?"

"I'm sure I wouldn't know." There were new lines in her face now—lines that were tight and bitter and angry. In the dim light of the shadowy room I could see her lips trembling ever so slightly.

I got out another cigarette and rolled it around in my fingers. "I don't like to insist," I told her. "But I'm the one who has to find your daughter. The trail can start anywhere. I don't work for a newspaper. What I find out when I'm working stays with me until my work is done. Then I forget it—all of it, Mrs. Fremont. I'd like you to understand that."

"No." Just as firmly and just as flatly. "It wouldn't help you. I know my daughter and I know *her*."

She meant it, too. I sighed and put the cigarette in my mouth and lighted it. "I guess that does it, Mrs. Fremont. I'll do what I can and keep you posted." I stood up and smiled my professional smile to indicate the interview was over.

They went with me into the tiny front hall, its air heavy with the smell of furniture polish. I took my hat off the old-fashioned combination wall rack and mirror and went over to the door. We said good-by and the old man gave me a hand the color and texture of Billy the Kid's saddle and mumbled something I didn't catch. I moved the hand up and down and returned it to him and went out to the vine-covered porch where a green porch swing crouched crossways on the narrow planks. It seemed the right place to spend the long summer evenings listening to the crickets and watching the snails whizz past.

The Fremonts said good-by a second time and Clara closed the door with its thin white dimity curtains behind an oval of glass. I walked slowly down the three wooden steps and on out to the curb of the quiet sun-baked street where the Plymouth waited.

I leaned on the car door and dropped my cigarette into the nice clean gutter there. I ran the nails of my left hand lightly along one cheek and looked back at the neat square little house among its rose bushes and freshly cut lawn.

Two nice old people in that house. I wondered what I'd have for them the next time I came to sit in their parlor and fill the draperies with the smell of my cigarettes. If I ever did.

I crawled in behind the wheel and drove away.

CHAPTER 2

It was getting on toward three o'clock. The sun was very bright and very hot, although this was nearly the end of September, and there was no breeze to speak of. I drove slowly on, sniffing at the strangely pleasant odor of what I finally decided was fresh air. They didn't have air like that in Chicago. They hardly had air there at all—just gas fumes with soft-coal smoke to give it body.

I spent more time than I intended, rolling along the clean wide streets, looking out at tall trees with leaves beginning to turn colors and at neat picket fences that might have been painted yesterday for all I could tell and at street markers that were legible and not bent at impossible angles.

And along the streets were houses. Houses instead of apartment buildings like the side of a cliff, and a flunky in uniform to open your car door and sneer at your taste in clothing, and a potted evergreen on each side of the entrance to furnish a touch of the forest primeval. Clean cool-looking houses with people in them who would know the people next door and go over and visit with them evenings and talk in a leisurely way about things beside money.

At Sixteenth and O streets I parked alongside a drugstore and went in and asked the clerk at the cigar counter for a telephone book. He said pleasantly that there was a booth at the rear and I walked back there between rows of sparkling display cases and found the book dangling at the end of a chain.

Nobody named Rehak was listed in it. I entered the booth and dumped a nickel in the proper slot and tried Information. She didn't have the name on her records either, but she was so nice about it I wanted to drop in a quarter just for her.

I came back to the front of the store, took a stool at the soda fountain and drank a malted milk while I listened to the soft whir from a pair of overhead fans. I wondered if a reasonably respectable private dick could make ends meet in a town like this. It hardly seemed possible.

I took my fountain check over to the cash register and a tall thin man who looked as if his father might have been a farmer rang it up and gave me my change.

"You wouldn't know a family named Rehak, would you?" I asked.

He chewed the name over silently, looking past me, a prominent Adam's apple twitching under the loose skin of his throat. "Well now, it don't seem so. Not right offhand."

"Is there such a thing as a city directory around?"

He went off on another thinking spree, elbows on the counter, the front of his white jacket bunched up. The gnawed barrel of a black fountain pen hung from the lip of an upper pocket.

"B'lieve there is," he rumbled. "Old one though. They ain't been puttin' 'em out lately. War and all."

"An old one might do the trick," I said. "Could I take a look at it? If it's no trouble."

"Why, no trouble at all." He straightened up and sounded cordial. "Might take a minute to find it. If you don't mind waitin'."

I said that was good of him and to take his time. He ambled down the store and out of sight behind a partition. I leaned a hip against the counter and tried reading the fine print on a Lydia Pinkham carton on one of the wall shelves.

Presently the druggist came back and handed me a not very robust volume between hard covers. I carried it over to one of the tables and leafed through to the R section. Halfway down one of the columns a Stanley Rehak was listed as owning a residence at 322 South Twentieth. He was the only Rehak shown.

I copied down the name and address and left the book next to the cash register and went on out into O Street. From what little I'd learned about the way Lincoln was laid out, the 300 block on South Twentieth should be a short drive from where I was now.

It was the only thread I had, really. Laura Fremont's last known address was nearly a year behind her. A trail that ancient could be as cold as a barefoot Eskimo. Chicago was six hundred miles away—not as far as the moon but too far for coming back for something I could have picked up the first time out.

I winked at a passing blonde, just to be neighborly, and got back into the Plymouth.

They had a dairy on the east side of South Twentieth—a low, tan-brick building that ran the full length of the block. A slow-moving mechanic in coveralls was fooling with the electric motor of a cream-colored home-delivery truck in one of the driveways. From the open windows behind him came the grind and rattle of a bottling machine.

Across from the dairy was a row of ancient frame dwellings of one and two stories, all of them empty of pride since a long time past. I pushed open a wire gate held shut by a rope weighted with scrap iron and went along the walk to the porch of a moldering gray bungalow. A rusted tin mailbox, once black, was nailed next to an equally rusted screen door that had long since stopped being a problem to the flies. No name on the mailbox and no mail in it. But tacked to the wood underneath were three shiny tin numbers that said this was *322.* It seemed unlikely that anyone would care.

I tried the screen door, found it hooked from the inside and pounded the heel of one hand against its frame. A piece of the stripping flew off and hit the porch at my feet. Nothing else happened, nobody answered my knock, nobody peered out from behind the drawn roller shades at the windows.

I rapped again. This time a thick voice from inside the house bellowed words I didn't understand. A full minute later the door opened and a man was standing in the thin gloom looking out at me. He was barefoot, wearing trousers with baggy knees, no shirt and from the waist up gray underwear with half-length sleeves.

I said, "Mr. Rehak? Stanley Rehak?"

His face was a Slavic face, hardly any meat on it, heavy cheekbones and a pinched-in jaw. The mouth hung open a little from long habit, loose-lipped. Blue eyes that were sunken and dull; coarse black hair standing up in tufts. More hair stuck out of his ears, like miniature fans.

"Yeah," he grunted. Phlegm rattled in his throat. "Wha'ya want?"

"A couple of questions I'd like to ask. Okay?"

He took awhile making up his mind. A thumb came up and dug into the underwear above his right hip. The sunken eyes sorted out the muscles of my face. His scowl was sleepy, neither friendly nor unfriendly.

The eyes shifted. He lifted a squat-fingered hand and fumbled off the screen's hook. "Yeah. You come in. I was sleeping." He made it sound tough and reproachful at the same time.

I stepped in and followed him through a square arch into a small living room. The furniture was as mismatched as furniture can get and hardly any of it. The floor was bare, the wood's original color long since lost under layers of ingrained dust. A floor lamp with a dime-store paper shade leaned at a drunken angle next to a maple settee with stained plaid upholstery that looked as comfortable to sit on as armor plate.

He went over and snapped up one of the shades, flooding the room with harsh light. He jerked a thumb at an unpainted kitchen chair and dropped onto the settee. I sat down where he had pointed and revolved my hat between my palms and breathed in the damp odor of decay that filled the room.

He clawed at his hair and wiped his nose with the back of a hand and eyed me with as much curiosity as he would ever have for anything.

"Hot like hell, hah?" he said thickly. He hawked suddenly, making it sound like a dirty sheet being torn, and spat on the floor. He was polite about it, turning his head first. "I don't wake up yet for maybe two hours. I am night watchman over to Strayer's."

He didn't say who or what Strayer's was. I didn't ask him. "Sorry I woke you, Mr. Rehak. It *is* hot. I'll ask my questions and run along and let you get back to bed."

He sat with his legs wide apart, wrists resting limply against his thighs, hands drooping between his legs, bare feet flat against the floor. They were gray feet with a slight crusting of dirt around the thick tendon above the heel. His face held all the interest and animation of a butcher's block. He was waiting for what I had to say.

"It's about your daughter," I said.

"Gracie?" A spark moved in his eyes. "I don't hear about her for long time now. Bertha Lund send you over, hah?"

"Who's Bertha Lund?"

He stared at me dully, not hearing the question or not

wanting to hear it. I blew out my breath and said, "I hear Gracie's in Chicago these days."

One of the hands moved slowly up along a thigh, scratched, moved as slowly down again. "Maybe. I kick her ass out long time ago. She's no good, mister. All the time men. Anything in pants. You a cop, hah?"

"Nothing like that, Mr. Rehak. There's another girl. She's missing and her folks want her found. I thought maybe Gracie might know where she's at."

He clenched and unclenched his toes. They moved slowly as if doing it gave him a secret kind of pleasure. He seemed to have forgotten me. I started to say something, but before I could get my mouth open he spoke.

"Cops used to call up all the time after the old lady died. 'We got your girl, Mr. Rehak,' they say. 'Selling herself on the street again, Mr. Rehak. You wanta come down bail her out?' I get her home and beat hell outa her. No good. Start all over again."

He wasn't talking to me, really. I put my hat on my knee and got out a cigarette. He watched me light it, uncaring, not actually seeing me. He might have been suffering or he might have been dozing. I couldn't tell which, if either.

I said, "I don't know a thing about Gracie, Mr. Rehak, and I don't have to. She may be in a position to clear up a small matter. If you could tell me where she's living in Chicago, or give me the name of someone who might know, I'd appreciate it."

Nothing changed in his face or in the dull way his eyes were watching me. But slowly the hands resting against his thighs began to knot into fists.

"Go away," he mumbled in a voice that matched his eyes. "I don't talk about her no more. Go the hell away, mister. I don't know who you are. I don't care who you are. She ain't here, mister. If she come here I kill her. Just go away, mister. Quick."

He closed his eyes and something glistened on the coarse skin below them. He sat like that, not moving, carved out of stone, while the knives of memory cut him apart inside.

I stood up silently and put on my hat, went into the hall and out the door.

CHAPTER 3

At a quarter past four I wandered into the lobby of my hotel, picked up the key at the desk and rode up to the room they'd given me when I arrived in town early that same morning.

I locked the door and shucked off my coat and hat and dropped them on the green-and-white candlewick bedspread. Cold air coming in through a vent high up in one wall had chilled the room beyond comfort. I closed the screen on it and went into the shining bathroom to strip down and stand awhile under a luke-warm shower, thinking about nothing at all.

The malted milk had buried what little appetite I might have had earlier. I got into trousers and a shirt, leaving the shirt unbuttoned and hanging, sat down at the phone and asked for Room Service.

I got the bell captain instead. His was a young voice and not loaded with the cynical grade of boredom common among bellhops.

"There's water in the tap," I said, "but I'm still thirsty. What can be done about it?"

"You want some hard likker, sir?"

"I accept your invitation," I said. "Bourbon will be fine. Soda and ice—and now."

He took my room number and said he would do what could be done. I stood up to lean against the window frame and watch the trickle of traffic along Twelfth Street. The town's skyscraper, twelve floors of dark-gray stone, stood tall and solid almost directly across the street. Behind one of the windows an elderly dentist in a white coat was pushing tools into a patient's mouth.

A knock at the door—a discreet knock, as though the party behind it was up to something not quite legitimate. I crossed over and turned the catch. A youngster about college age came in with an aluminum tray covered with a white cloth. I pointed to the writing desk and he let the tray down on it and took off the cloth. A pint of bonded bourbon, two bottles of charged water, ice cubes in a glass bucket, an opener for the bottles, two highball glasses in case I had company.

"Very pretty," I remarked. "Do I sign something?"

"Yes, sir." He slid a freckled hand under the lapel of his natty gray-blue uniform coat and brought out a ruled square of cardboard with amounts stamped in purple ink. I wrote my name across the bottom with his pencil and gave them back to him, with half a dollar.

He thanked me and was on his way to the door when I thought of something. I said, "Hold it. What's the penalty in Nebraska for contributing to the delinquency of a minor?"

He stood there with his arms hanging down and his eyebrows trying to climb into a thatch of reddish hair. He tried out a smile but the corners sagged on him. "Well now, I wouldn't rightly know, sir. That's quite a question."

"It only sounded that way," I said. "I was thinking of offering you a drink but I wouldn't want to be arrested for it."

"Oh." His weak smile became a shy grin. "Why, that's all right, sir. I was twenty-one nearly two months back."

That gave me twelve years on him. But at fifteen I had

been older than he was now. "Congratulations," I said. "Now you can run for alderman." I pointed the neck of the bourbon bottle at the easy chair. "Sit down. This calls for a celebration."

He came slowly back to perch on the chair's edge, watching me open the whisky and remove the cap on one of the soda bottles. I put together a pair of modest drinks, handed him one and sat on the bed. We lifted the glasses and drank. It wasn't the best bourbon, yet adequate for a man of my simple tastes.

He refused a cigarette but struck a match for mine. His hands had a scrubbed look and the nails were filed to the quick. I leaned back against the headboard and drew up my bare feet. I had soaped them twice while under the shower. Especially around the ankles.

I said, "I came across a name this afternoon. The way I heard it makes me think it might be more than just a private party. Maybe hearing it would mean something to you."

He nodded in an expressionless, man-of-the-world manner and tossed off another gulp out of his glass. It didn't quite come off the way he had hoped. His homely face twisted a little as the bourbon went down. He took his nose out of the glass and gulped some air, his eyes watering.

"It might, sir," he said gravely. "What was the name?"

"A woman's name," I said. "Bertha Lund."

His cheeks burned suddenly and some of the friendliness left his face. "I've heard about her," he said tonelessly.

I waited for more. He sat turning his glass and looking everywhere except at me. After an interval of that, I set my glass on the floor and got out my wallet. I removed a couple of limp-looking dollar bills and held them loosely in one hand where he could see them. "Tell me about Bertha Lund a little," I said.

He stared at the money. Not in a way that said he wanted it. "She owns a tavern," he said softly. "Out on Thirtieth and Merrill."

"Uh-hunh," I said when he stopped there. "That'll do for a starter but it's not two bucks' worth."

"You don't have to give me a cent," he retorted with a quiet dignity. "All I know is what I've heard, and you're welcome to it. They say Bertha Lund runs a house—if you know what I mean. But that's only part of it. You hear all kinds of talk. I heard stories that things go on out there I wouldn't even talk about. And I been around, too."

I stared at him until patches of color began to burn in his plain and artless face. "And this seemed such a nice town," I said. "Clean air and shimmering stone and a big blue sky. Empty jails and very little garbage and no roaring traffic's boom. I ought to punch you one right in the nose."

His mouth was open. "What's the matter with you, mister?"

"Matter? Nothing's the matter. How can you say that? Everything's right. As right as two left feet in a wall bed on a purple-tinged morning in May. What were you saying?"

He seemed to be retreating deeper into the chair and his glass shook a little in his hand. He wanted to be up and away. Away anywhere as long as it was away from this room. I got off the bed and went into the bathroom and threw my cigarette into the bowl.

When I came out again he was standing in the center of the rug, holding his half-filled glass like it was too heavy for him. I went over and pushed the two dollars into his unoccupied fingers. His character got in the way and he said, "Thank you," before he realized he was saying it.

"I asked you," I said, "and you told me. Thirtieth and Merrill. Is that right?"

"Yes, sir."

"A tavern, you said?"

"Yes, sir. Sign says 'Marty's'."

"How do I get there?"

He thought. "Well, you go out O Street east to Twenty-seventh, then north to Merrill. About the twenty-two hundred block that way. Thirtieth would be another three blocks east." He shook his head almost regretfully, like the local chamber of commerce getting ready to make an admission. "You won't like it out there, mister. A bad district after dark. But then night's the only time you'll find anybody around."

I took the glass away from him and got rid of it. He smiled shyly and smoothed the two bills he was still holding and put them deep in a pocket and waited for me to tell him he could run along.

I said, "If I need you again, who do I ask for?"

"Chester, sir. Chester Weedlow."

"It goes down in my book."

"Uh—thanks for the drink, mister."

"You hardly touched it."

"And the two dollars."

"Just saying hello to you was worth that much."

He had no idea what I was talking about. I hardly knew myself. He said something polite, sidled to the door and out, closing the door like it might blow up in his face. A town with even one bellhop like Chester had to be all anybody could ask for.

I leaned against the window frame and looked out and thought my thoughts. I lighted a cigarette and bounced the folder of matches on my palm. The cover had a cut of the hotel on it, looking as tall as Rockefeller Center and twice as imposing. I put them in my pocket, went over and mixed another drink and carried it back to the window.

I stood there a long, long time. Dusk slowly filled the street below and began to crawl in at the window. The sky lost its hot look and became a soft faraway gray. A red neon sign in a haberdashery across the way came on and threw a harsh pattern of color across the walk.

Finally I looked at my strap watch. Still several hours before I could put Plan X into operation. I moved my coat off the bed, pushed up the pillows and stretched out with my glass and a cigarette and a mind filled with drifting thoughts. . . .

CHAPTER 4

MERRILL STREET. Old bricks down the center, with holes to knock your wheels out of line or snap a spring. Big naked electric globes on top of iron poles, with flat tin reflectors above them to push the light down against cracked, uneven sidewalks.

Weathered frame houses in need of paint they would never get crouched in narrow plots of hard naked earth or among dried-out patches of brown grass littered with paper and empty cans and the broken remains of toys. Once in a while a withered tree, black branches thrust starkly skyward as though praying for the rain they could no longer use.

The neighborhood youth moved aimlessly through the shadows of the hot airless streets or stood in loose groups at intersections, twirling key chains and talking in short sentences that came out wrapped in smoke from their cigarettes. Men in undershirts sat drinking beer on top steps of sagging porches, and the voices of slatternly women were shrill against the night.

At the corner of Thirtieth a vertical electric sign that read MARTY'S stuck out over the walk from the second floor of a two-story building of time-corroded red brick. Faded green blinds were drawn in the upstairs windows. Downstairs was a double store-front window with the word BEER in green neon script against a backdrop of white cheesecloth.

At a few minutes past ten I parked across the street from the tavern, rolled up the windows and got out. I was thorough about locking doors. Cars were strung along both curbs, not all of them in the low-price field.

The entrance to Marty's was set in a shallow recess and stood open to the night's dry heat. Juke-box jive rolled out through it carrying the reek of fermented hops. Four men near the window were suddenly silent as I came toward them. It was the silence of a prison yard as the head screw walks by.

I moved past them and their brand of silence and on into the half-light found in barrooms everywhere. A single room, long and narrow and low-ceilinged. No plush, no chrome, and the only mirror a smeared length behind unimaginative displays of whisky and gin bottles in back of a darkwood bar. The opposite wall held a line of booths in the same wood, and all the way back were two closed doors flanking a juke box bright with swirling colors.

Not at all what I expected. No grog-mill cuties with peekaboo blouses and boudoir keys ready in sweating palms. No slim-waisted junker with a snapbrim hat and a deck of nose candy for sale to the right guy. Not even one B-girl behind her shot glass of cold tea.

Just men in shirt sleeves drinking beer out of the standard kind of glassware, and in the booths matronly housewives doing the same thing and maybe talking about eggs and flour and the iceman taking an hour to drop off fifty pounds at Mrs. Ramsey's.

I found a place at the bar and one of the aprons came along and asked my pleasure. He was a middle-aged giant with a face like a peat bog and the same amount of wavy black hair you find on a lightning rod.

"Whisky sour," I said.

He blinked lashless eyes. "Sorry, Spike. Not that I wouldn't want to, y'understand. But we got a law says no. Somebody should of told ya."

I pointed at the bottle goods. "What about them? Or are you waiting for repeal?"

He didn't bother to turn his head. "Don't mean a thing, Spike. Empties, see. You gotta put something behind a bar else it don't look like no bar. Catch on?"

"A beer, then," I said. "And a word with Bertha Lund."

He frowned ponderously. "This is Marty's, Spike. Like the sign says. You want beer, huh?"

"When I want beer, I'll ask for beer. Get word to Bertha she's got company. And how about that beer I ordered?"

He took hold of his side of the bar with both hands. I could hear the wood creak. "One beer," he said in a strangled way. He turned and went along the bar and pressed a button below one of the cash registers. When he came back there was a glass of beer in one of his paws. He put it in front of me and took my dime and rang it up. He almost snapped the key on the register ringing it up.

I lighted a cigarette and drank some of the foam in my glass and listened to the juke box yell about love. One of the matrons upset her beer and caught most of it in her ample lap. She said a few choice words that crackled like the weighted tip of a mule whip and came over to the bar for a towel.

A hand touched my elbow gently. It was a soft meaty hand, like a lily pad, and was attached to a small pale man in a dark suit, white shirt and figured blue necktie. He looked like a Lithuanian janitor on his Sunday off, until you saw his eyes and smelled the acrid smoke of marijuana on his breath.

"I'm Marty," he murmured. "You wanted something?"

"Not from you," I said. "It was a lady I had in mind."

"No girlies here." He smiled dreamily up at me. But he

was really thousands of miles away. Away on a tropical isle below the equator, with dancing girls and fat eunuchs and long-handled peacock fans waved by ebon slaves. "Just a quiet place to have a beer and listen to the pretty music."

"I'll bet," I said. I made a sniffing sound. "Nice grade of tea you're wearing there, Marty."

His distant dark eyes were suddenly sharp and direct. His voice cut through the clink of glassware, the clang of cash registers, the vibrating notes of the record player. "What's your business, mister? I don't have all day."

"I want a few words with Bertha," I said, "about a small matter that won't do anything to her one way or the other. If that won't unlock her door, say it's about a girl she used to know."

He didn't nod, but he didn't shake his head either. He said, "Stick around," and floated on down the room, all the way down and through one of the doors next to the juke box. He used a key to get the door open. It didn't have to mean anything that he used a key.

Some time went by. I finished my beer. I would have ordered another if the apron had suggested it. But he never came near me.

Presently the rear door opened and Marty looked into the bar. He caught my eye and motioned with his head. I went back there and followed him through, along a short hall with naked plaster walls and up a steep flight of steps with rubber treads.

We came into a narrow corridor with the same bare plaster walls. Paneled doors on either side were painted a hideous brown. Most of the doors were closed. A young colored girl, carrying a stack of towels, squeezed past us, giving me a secret smile. She wore a white wrap-around apron and had legs like toothpicks. In the air was an odor of strong soap and disinfectant. Not a nice odor at all.

It was none of my business what the place smelled like. I trailed the little man to a white door at the corridor's far end. He knocked twice and a baritone voice said, "All right," and we went through.

CHAPTER 5

THIS was a room to remember, to hurt your eyes, to make you open your veins for the sake of a little color. The all-over rug was a shaggy twist in pure white, the walls a pale cream, the windows hidden behind eggshell draperies and Venetian blinds in glistening white. One wall held a pair of snowscapes in frames of white pebbled leather that matched three pull-up chairs in the general vicinity of an executive-sized desk painted a warm ivory. Everything on the desk, from the blotter to the telephone, was a neutral shade.

It was like stepping into a bottle of milk.

Sitting behind the desk and looking at me without much interest was a woman in a dark-green blouse and a severe gray suit with white pinstripes. She was a big woman, shoulders broad and square and a lot of bosom that seemed to be in one piece. Her black hair was straight and coarse and cut like that of the third cellist in the London Philharmonic. Just by sitting there she gave the impression of being able to break the javelin-throw record any afternoon of the week.

She waved a large ringless hand at the chair nearest my side of the desk. "Be seated, sir. I won't need you, Marty."

The door closed without a sound, leaving me alone with Bertha Lund. I sat down and crossed my legs and stared frankly at her. She was the kind of woman you had to throw your weight at right away or get no place with. She was smoking a cigarette in a short ivory holder and staring back at me. Her eyes were hard and brown under bushy black brows. Her face was full and handsome in the way a man's face is handsome and was completely free of make-up. It was a face that would let you know its secrets—if you used scopolamine and three sticks of dynamite.

She said, "Marty didn't catch your name."

"Marty," I said, "couldn't catch a ping-pong ball with a wash tub."

She hadn't expected that kind of approach. Her mouth hardened. "If you've got a chip on your shoulder just walk right on out. I didn't send for you."

"I worked too hard getting in," I said, grinning. "The name is Pine."

She brushed a few crumbs of tobacco from the white blotter with the side of her hand and looked thoughtfully at the points of my display handkerchief. Smoke from her cigarette claimbed straight up in the room's still air. Slowly her first rush of anger faded, leaving the face smooth once more.

"Stranger in town, Mr. Pine?"

"That's right."

"How do you like our little city?"

"I like it fine."

She nodded as though I'd said the only thing to be said. "A town of retired farmers, largely. A university town, pretty much on the quiet side. I wouldn't trade it for a hundred New Yorks."

"Even if they threw in Cleveland?" I said.

Her thick brows joined to make a puzzled scowl. "What's Cleveland got to do with it?"

"No more than New York," I said.

She twitched one shoulder and put the ivory holder in a groove of a white plastic ash tray. She bent sideways over the white leather arm of her chair and tugged open a bottom drawer and brought out two shot glasses and a bottle of Black Label. It seemed the wrong brand of Scotch for this room.

She filled both glasses to the brim with practiced ease and pushed one over to me. Evidently I impressed her as a man who would want his liquor straight. We drank and she smacked her lips louder than I did. She returned the bottle to the drawer, kicked it shut with a hard motion of her foot, leaned back in the chair and swung one leg over the other. Her smile was as guarded as her eyes and her eyes were as guarded as the Philadelphia Mint.

She said, "I'm Bertha Lund. What was it you wanted? Something about a girl, Marty said."

"A girl you used to know," I said. "I hear she's in Chicago these days. I want to find her."

"Why?" Straight out. Direct. The way a man would have said it.

"I need a piece of information. I think she can furnish it."

"Is this a personal matter? Or what?"

"Nothing personal. A job of work to me. I have a client."

Her brown eyes were very still, very careful. Her bosom rose and fell under slow breathing. "A client," she repeated softly. "What are you—a lawyer?"

I got out my wallet and slid a business card across the white blotter. She used a thumb and forefinger to pick it up by the edges. She read the words without moving her lips, no expression marring the strong lines of her face.

"Private dick," she said tonelessly. "Well." She spread her fingers and the card plopped soundlessly against the blotter. "Who gave you my name?"

"It came up kind of indirectly, Miss Lund."

She lifted the ivory holder and pushed it between her lips. A long feather of curling smoke floated ceilingward as she tilted back her chin to let me see the stocky lines of her muscular neck.

"You've got one hell of a nerve," she said suddenly. "You practically muscle your way in here and demand information. But I don't notice you giving out any. Private cops aren't new to me, Pine. I've met them before. A shady, seedy pack, full of wind and backed up by a nickel's worth of authority."

A lot of words but nothing in them for me. I looked back at her and said nothing.

She said, "All right. Who are you working for?"

"My client, Miss Lund."

"And who might that be?"

"You wouldn't know him."

The hard brown eyes gleamed like pebbles in a river bed. "How would you know who I wouldn't know? That will be all, Mr. Pine. I don't have information for any cop—private or public."

She leaned forward to reach a forefinger under the edge of the desk. I said, "Before you ring for the runner, think what turning me out empty-handed can mean."

"To me," she snapped, "not a thing." She sounded like she meant it. But the finger didn't go any farther.

I worked a cigarette from my pack, lighting it with a match from the folder the hotel had furnished. Bertha Lund watched my hands, frowning, thinking behind the frown. I waved out the match and dropped it into the white tray and leaned back again. I said, "From the way you've been biting my neck, I'd say you know where Gracie Rehak can be found. You can tell me, and now, or I can ask the local law to put pressure where pressure will count. If they can't get it out of you, putting some of your two-dollar broads through the wringer might help. I want what I want, Miss Lund, and somebody in this bird cage is going to give it to me."

She was staring at me with her mouth open. "Gracie Rehak? Good Christ, is *that* who you're talking about?"

"Who did you have in mind?" I said.

She wasn't listening. "Little Gracie. Well, well. What's that flat-chested kitten been up to?"

"I wouldn't know, Miss Lund."

She seemed greatly relieved—almost too relieved for me to believe I had removed a weight from her mind. She avoided my eyes while working the butt of her cigarette out of the ivory holder. She used a burned matchstick to press out the coal, wiped her fingers on a man's handkerchief from a desk drawer and put it away again.

The smooth lack of expression was back on her face by the time she was through with all that. She got out of her chair, said, "Excuse me a moment, Mr. Pine. I may be able to help you after all."

She moved around the corner of the desk and past me with a long smooth stride, to the door and out, closing it softly at her back.

It might have been to order up the heavy artillery or to take a cake out of the oven. It might even have been for the reason she gave. Either of the first two seemed more likely.

I rose and walked around behind the desk and stood there looking at the closed drawers. No point in going through them, even if I had the time, which I doubted. The handsome white leather swivel chair stood on a white rubber mat protecting the white rug. Just the room to have anemia in. I rubbed the sole of my shoe against the mat for no reason, then turned and went back to my chair.

Bertha Lund came in almost immediately afterward. She crossed to her chair with her free-wheeling stride. She picked up the empty ivory holder and held it lengthwise in front of her and looked over it at me, resting her elbows on the blotter. "Dead end, I'm afraid," she said casually. "I tried getting Gracie's address from a girl who knew her well in the old days. Seems she hasn't heard from Gracie since the day she left town."

"And I had such hopes," I said solemnly. "Does that mean I'm to say thanks and crawl out the door?"

"I didn't say that."

"You haven't said anything."

Her lips formed a white furious line. "Get out of here, you cheap tin star! Before you get thrown out on your can!"

We sat and glared at each other across the ivory expanse of desk. But I had more practice at being glared at and finally she looked past me at the layers of smoke hanging in the still air.

She said stiffly, "Don't ever think you can't stretch that tough-guy act too far with me. This is my neck of the woods and I can get away with more than you might imagine."

"My imagination has no limits, Miss Lund. Why talk about it?"

She sighed. "I suppose," she said with weary patience, "the way to get rid of you is to tell you what little I can about Gracie. She left Lincoln three years or so ago. I've heard from her two or three times since. The last was that she might go to New York." She nodded slowly. "As it happens, I had a card from her from there."

"When was that?"

"Hell, how would I know? I threw the card away." She took a cigarette from a white plastic box near the ivory telephone and screwed it into the ivory holder. "Must be all of a year ago."

"No more than a year?"

She clamped strong white teeth around the holder and struck a match with her thumbnail. "It might be." She blew a thick streamer of smoke between us and waved it away. Light from the overhead fixture glinted dully on the unpainted nails. "I can't be sure."

"She might have gone back to Chicago since then," I suggested.

"Sure. Or even South America. They like her type down there, I hear."

"What was her type?"

She looked blank for a moment. I said tiredly, "I don't mean her type of work. I'm asking for a description of her. Or did you throw that away, too?"

She said hotly, "I've had about all of you I'm——" She stopped abruptly and bit down on the holder. "Gracie was small, black-haired, dark brown eyes. Figure like a boy's. Pretty in a weak, helpless sort of way. Men with large forceful wives found her very appealing."

"Somebody must know more than that about her," I said. "Her family, for instance."

"I never knew her people."

"Anyone at all you can suggest I see?"

"No one at all, Mr. Pine. I'm so sorry."

I uncrossed my legs, stood up, took my hat off a corner of the desk and put it on my head. "Thanks for not a goddam thing," I growled. "You've sat there and fed me a pack of lies—and not out of natural meanness alone. I'd say you don't want Gracie Rehak found. I'm going to find her, Miss Lund, and I hope enough dynamite comes out of finding her to blow you out of this cathouse and into pokey. It will be a pleasure. Good night to you, Miss Lund."

Her mouth was a wolf trap and two spots of color flared in her cheeks. Very carefully she put the cigarette down and then very quickly she jerked open the center drawer of the desk and brought out a small black gun.

The gun was still coming up when I leaned down across the desk. I locked a set of fingers around her thick wrist and banged it sharply against the wood and the gun fell back into the open drawer. It was in my hand and I had straightened up before she caught her breath.

I listened to her swear in a dry monotone like the buzz of

a rattler. When she started repeating herself my interest died. "You left out one of my uncles," I said. "But he never amounted to much anyway. Get the pimple, sister. I need to get out in the fresh air."

"Give—me—that—gun!"

"How would you like picking it out of your teeth?"

She stabbed blindly at the buzzer. Her hand shook until I seemed to hear the bones rattle. Thirty seconds of silence as tight as a piano wire before a small knock at the door. Marty put his head in. "Yeah, Bertha?"

Her expression was the only answer he got. It was answer enough. His eyes swiveled to me. He saw the gun in my hand and jumped slightly. I motioned for him to come all the way in. I patted his pockets and under the arms. He had no more gun than a penguin. The room was so quiet I could hear him breathe.

I said, "These things always turn out like the second feature at the Bijou. Shooting me would have been unsmart, Miss Lund. I think you just wanted to scare me a little, hunh?"

She moved her lips but nothing came through them. I looked down at the gun in my hand. A Colt .25 automatic. Deadly across the width of a desk in the hand of a marksman. I took out my handkerchief and covered my fingers while emptying the magazine and the remaining shell in the chamber. I snapped the magazine back into place and tossed the gun onto the nice white carpet. It hit with a dull *thunk*, bounced once and came to rest.

"Thanks for having me in, Miss Lund," I said. "I may drop you a bread-and-butter note one of these days. If I can find any white ink."

It didn't bring down the house. Neither of them moved while I was closing the door on my way out.

CHAPTER 6

IT WASN'T much past eleven o'clock when I parked the car a block north of the hotel. The city had turned in for the night. A pedestrian or two moved along the silent length of Twelfth Street, and in the pale-yellow glow from a coffee-shop window a cab driver leaned against a lamp post and picked at his teeth with thoughtful care.

Only one of the hotel elevators was operating at this hour. A sleepy bellhop ran me up to the fourth floor, muttered, "Good night, sir," and was dropping out of sight before the door clanged shut.

I stood in the dim and empty corridor, getting out my room key tied to an oval of maroon fiberboard and listening to the whir of the descending cage and the sound of water running in a shower stall close by. It had been a long evening, a disappointing evening, even a dirty evening. The smell of Bertha Lund's place of business was still bitter in my nostrils. I lighted a cigarette, dropped the match into a sand jar and went on down the hall to 421.

I had the door open and was reaching for the wall switch when the blow caught me. I must have made a wonderful target. I didn't even have a chance to yell.

"On the head," I said. "It always happens to the back of your head. You ought to wear a Bessemer steel hat."

I giggled into the rug. Bessemer steel. Will a ton be

enough, sir? That's a mighty big head you got there. Two tons? Thank you, sir. Shall I wrap it up or will you wear it?

I opened my eyes. Bright specks floated and darted like a school of minnows through a velvet ocean. Black velvet. Only five yards to a customer during our special sale.

I blinked away the specks and pushed up until I was on my hands and knees. The carpet was hot and gritty under my palms. I started to crawl. I was as weak as a three-card flush. I kept on crawling. My head banged into the side of the bed. I got over the shock of that and managed to get up on the mattress. The Alps would have been colder but not as high. I lay there panting, feeling the bed, the room, the hotel, the universe—all revolving.

Some time passed. More than five minutes but less than two weeks. I reached for the headboard and pulled myself up and leaned against it. More time passed. I thought about turning on a light. A matter of getting on my feet and strolling over to the desk and finding the lamp. I could do it. I would do it—after a while.

I stood up. The blackness lurched, steadied, lurched again. The window was a pattern of horizontal stripes in alternate black and gray. That would be the Venetian blind, lowered but not completely closed. No reddish tinge to the darkness beyond it. The haberdasher across the street had turned off his sign. A penny saved was a penny earned.

Enough of this. I wavered across the room to where the desk should be. My hand was already out to find the lamp there. My fingers brushed its shade. And the toe of my shoe thudded against something firm yet yielding.

A long frozen pause. No sound in the room except tortured breathing. Mine. I leaned both hands against the desk, not looking down, and slid my foot carefully along the length of whatever it had hit against.

Just turn the lamp button and you'll know. I didn't want to turn the button. I already knew. I wanted to walk out of this dark room, out of the hotel, over to my car and away. What about your bags? The hell with my bags! A suit and a few shirts and some uninitialed underwear. And socks—don't forget the socks. The hell with the socks, too!

I turned the button.

He lay on his side, knees bent, arms straight down. The snappy gray-blue uniform was no longer snappy and the upper part no longer gray-blue. The face was the face of Chester Weedlow, but behind that was a red-and-gray smear instead of a head.

Three fast strides got me into the bathroom. The bowl was waiting, its lids up. I vomited. They must have heard me in Detroit.

Years later I straightened up and pushed the lever. I sat on the edge of the tub until my legs stopped shaking and my hands were ready to obey orders. I stood up and turned on the bathroom light and found a glass on a shelf behind the mirror. I drank some water and smoked half a cigarette and looked at a gray strained face in the mirror. It was a face that needed a long vacation. I grunted and went back into the other room.

Both my bags were open and the contents scattered. The dresser drawers were pulled out and the stuff in them jumbled together. Nothing seemed to be missing. Nothing would be, unless it was clothing the guy had been hunting for. I doubted that. Then what? My wallet was still in my hip pocket. Money, identification, business cards—all in place. The envelope with the notations about Laura Fremont was pushed down behind the handkerchief in my breast pocket where I had put it hours before.

My hat was on the floor, its crown pushed in, a flattened

cigarette next to it. I bent and took up the hat and fumbled it back into shape while I stared at the cigarette. It had been lighted once but only a few puffs taken before a foot had snuffed it out. My brand. Probably the one I had lighted in the hall. It must have fallen out of my mouth when the sap landed. Somebody hadn't wanted the rug to be ruined. Blood and brains will wash out, but a cigarette burn is always bad.

The body still lay near the desk, in a shadow where the lamp rays didn't quite reach. Chester Weedlow. Twenty-one years were all he'd had. Through school and on into a job, such as it was. Then, with no warning and for no good reason, the end of the trail. Not that he cared any more. He was past caring. Maybe nobody would care—except me. And I couldn't prove a thing.

I ripped off the bedspread with savage hands and covered the body. The bourbon was still on the desk, tightly corked. It didn't appear to be loaded with arsenic. I took a long swallow without bothering to use a glass. It burned like a superior grade of carbolic acid after what my stomach had been through. But it gave me the strength to do what had to be done.

The telephone felt cool, even a trifle damp. Anger was beginning to rise in me. A dull anguished anger born of futility. A click came over the wire and the prissy voice of the night clerk said, "Operator."

"Get me the police," I said.

CHAPTER 7

IF CHICAGO had changed any during my five days away, it wasn't for the better. Traffic swore and grumbled in the canyons of the Loop, elevated trains screeched on the same sharp curves, pedestrians crossed blindly against the lights, and the sooty façades of towering buildings stood shoulder to shoulder with an air of hostile serenity.

I kept an office in the Clawson Building on East Jackson Boulevard. Two rooms on the eighth floor, the inner one fitted out with an oak desk and swivel chair, a couple of brown metal filing cabinets, one window and an atmosphere filled with the smell of damp plaster, aged cigarette smoke and one of the cleaning women's cologne.

There was an accumulation of mail on the linoleum under the letter drop. I scooped it up, raised the blind and the window beyond to let in the sounds of the city. A gray and white pigeon on the outside ledge gave me the beady eye, said, "Welcome home, Pine," and went away on pigeon business.

The mail amounted to nothing that couldn't have stayed on the floor another week. I lighted a cigarette, fished an address book from the windrows of junk in the center drawer, looked up David Ingram's office number and dialed it.

The girl put me through, after taking my name. A receiver went up and one of those voices too heavy for the telephone said, "Good morning, Paul. When did you get back?"

"About an hour ago," I told him. "Thought you'd like to know I'm working for the Fremonts."

"I'm interested, of course. What did Sweetland have to say?"

"About what you expected. The way I hear it, the two of you floated through college on bootleg alcohol and black coffee."

His chuckle shook the receiver. "Matt's quite a guy. As smart an attorney as you'd hope to find and a heart the size of his belly. This business of paying most of your fee for the Fremonts is an example."

"He told me about that," I said. "They were his first clients twenty-three years ago. Seems they were buying a house at the time and needed a fixer to read the fine print in the deed. They looked at his diploma in its shiny new frame, paid respectful attention to his law-school double talk, called him 'sir' and paid his fee with five sweat-soaked dollar bills.

"After that they always came to him with their problems. Theirs were simple problems and far apart: advice on insurance and a small argument over a special assessment the town pushed through one year. Then a couple weeks ago the old man came to him about the daughter being missing, which is how come he asked you to recommend a private dick. You suggested me and I thank you—I think."

"You *think*?" he said sharply. "What's wrong with the job, Paul? The Fremonts give you trouble?"

"They wouldn't give anyone trouble, Mr. Ingram. Their girl is gone and they're frantic in a genteel, sorry-to-trouble-you way. No. There's been a murder."

A deafening silence came from his end of the wire. I could picture him with his feet in Peal shoes up on the acre of mahogany desk in the large book-lined room with its thick wine-colored carpeting and oil portraits of Supreme Court justices.

"Paul."

"Yes, sir?"

"I'm exceedingly sorry if I've unwittingly been the cause of your being involved in anything . . . " The sentence was getting too complex and he let it taper off.

"Officially," I said, "I'm not involved. The Lincoln cops came up with the answer while buffing their nails. They think some prowler broke into my hotel room and was caught in the act by a bellboy, who lost half his head under a blackjack as a reward. They took my deposition and let me leave town. They almost yawned in my face it was that simple. The case; not my face."

"Only," Ingram said with slow emphasis, "it's not that simple. Is that what you're saying?"

"Uh-hunh. There's a dike named Bertha Lund out there who runs a poor man's bordello. I went out to get a line on a girl of hers who used to know Laura Fremont. I was careless enough to let Bertha see a book of matches from the hotel I was staying at. My guess is she sent someone to go through my luggage for a line on what I was up to. But I didn't tell that to the town whittlers. I had no proof to begin with, and they'd have asked questions I wouldn't have liked to answer."

The sound of his breathing rustled against my ear. In the office next to mine the fat little dentist was using his drill.

I went on talking, finishing it up. "I don't think any of this ties in with Laura Fremont. She once knew a girl who took the primrose path—if they still call it that. A girl who either doesn't want to be found or can't afford to be. Anyway, I thought you'd like to know how I made out."

He said he appreciated it and to let him know any new developments and we hung up. I sat there, one leg over a chair arm, and eyed the blonde on the Varga calendar above the filing cases. She was wearing very brief heliotrope overalls three degrees tighter than her skin, and from the looks of things had just come down from the haymow. I judged the hired man had gone back to his chores.

Looking at blondes would solve no problems. I took my leg off the chair and threw it under the desk and brought out the envelope with the few lines about Laura Fremont written on its back. I smoothed it out and laid it on the desk and smoothed it again. I thought of a hall with naked plaster walls separating closed doors. I thought of a young colored girl with a shy smile and an armload of towels. I smelled the smell of disinfectant and a brand of soap worse than the odor it was supposed to eliminate. I thought of a white web of a room with a fat spider of a woman in it. I remembered a hotel room clammy with the feel of air conditioning and on the floor a body with a slice of horror for a face and nothing behind the face except red and gray ooze.

My teeth bit into a knuckle. I said, "Ouch!" in a surprised voice. I picked up the envelope and read off the two addresses. YWCA, 814 North Dearborn Street. 1682 North LaSalle Street. Both would house working girls who were short on cash and long on hope. Both were in a frowzy district on the northern fringes of the Loop. The Y would be as antiseptic as a hospital corridor and with about the same amount of homelike atmosphere. But it would also have a file on tenants past and present.

The phone book listed several entries under YWCA. I called the one on North Dearborn and explained what I was after. The receiver made popping noises, a girlish voice said, ". . . keep his hands to himself, or—" followed by an abrupt and bottomless silence. While I was wondering if I was still with the YWCA or stranded somewhere off in an old conduit, a line opened and a briskly feminine voice said, "Miss Bryce speaking. May I help you?"

"More than likely," I said. "Awhile back you had a tenant

named Laura Fremont. I'd like her forwarding address."

"We are not permitted to give out such information, sir."

"My name is Cooper," I said. "With the Acme Chair Company." My tone indicated she was probably sitting on one of our products and if there was any more nonsense I'd come over and jerk it out from under her. "Rules are rules, Miss Bryce, and I understand you must observe them. But this isn't a matter of trying to collect a bill and I'm not a jealous suitor. About two years ago we promised Miss Fremont a position as soon as we opened a certain department in our organization—a position, I might add, she was most anxious to have. Unless I can locate her, we're going to have to fill that job elsewhere. Would you like to call me back on this?"

It was a reasonable story, not a flaw in it, the right words in the right tone. It went through Miss Bryce's guard like a thrown brick. She said, "Well, in that case . . . Will you hold the wire, Mr. Cooper?"

I said I'd be delighted and to take her time, and she went away to look in a file. I leaned back and listened to the Venetian-blind cords rattle against the window frame. A chill breeze was beginning to rise outside, making a lonesome wailing sound.

The receiver said, "I have that information, sir. 1682 North LaSalle Street."

"That's too bad," I said.

"I beg——"

"We know that address, Miss Bryce. She left there several months ago. I'd hoped she might have returned to the YWCA." I thought of something. "Tell me, the girls there sometimes share their rooms, don't they?"

"Why, yes. We——"

"Did Laura Fremont have a roommate?"

A pause while a paper rattled. "As a matter of fact, she did. A Mary Conrad. But she hasn't been with us for nearly two years."

"A forwarding address on her might help. You never know."

More papers rattled. "We show 470 Surf Street for her."

I scribbled it down on my calendar pad and was about to say something when she added, "That address is in care of Rehak, Mr. Cooper."

"That's fi—— Hunh?"

"Pardon?"

I wet my lips. "Never mind. A crocodile just went by. You said Rehak?"

"That is correct." Her voice was suddenly stiff with doubt. Chair company executives were never flippant. "Did you get the address, Mr. Cooper?"

"I got it," I said. "It nearly tore my glove off but I got it."

"What are you—?"

"Not the address," I said. "The address is peachy. I'll think of you every time I look at it. I certainly thank you, Miss Bryce. Isn't it a lovely day?"

She banged down her receiver. I laid mine gently back in its cradle and patted it affectionately and whistled two bars of "Dixie" through my teeth. In care of Rehak. Not a common name at all. Either Gracie Rehak was back in the picture or this was the Paul Bunyan of coincidence.

I copied onto the envelope the address Miss Bryce had been lied out of and, after it, the name Mary Conrad. The phone book showed a long list of Conrads but no Mary Conrad on or near Surf Street. A few Rehaks, mostly in the heavily Polish section on the town's southwest side. No Laura Fremont at all.

I folded the envelope small and neat and tucked it deep in

my wallet, then unlocked a file-cabinet drawer and got out my underarm holster, complete with gun, and strapped it on. A tribute to the kind of people Grace Rehak had known in the past and might still know today.

I emptied the ash tray into the wastebasket and was closing the window when I heard the corridor door open and close and light steps come into the reception room and stop there.

I had a visitor.

CHAPTER 8

He was standing in the center of the room, trying not to breathe in too much of its tainted air, eying the couch as if he might be thinking of sitting on it but hoping he wouldn't have to. From between two long slim fingers a cigarette sent up a wavering line of pale smoke.

He turned sharply, after I poked my head through the communicating door, and I got a long, hairline-to-socks inspection from cold blue eyes set in an oval, fair-skinned face that appeared to have been shaved on the way up in the elevator. He had smooth dark hair with a side part, a thin smallish nose, a narrow tight-lipped mouth. The chin didn't seem unusually aggressive but it wasn't backing away either.

"I gather you're Pine." The tone of his light husky voice said he would make an effort to tolerate me but I wasn't to expect any miracles.

"Uh-hunh. Come in and I'll dust off a chair."

I retreated behind the desk while he shrugged out of two hundred dollars' worth of tailored gray cashmere topcoat. Without it he was a long-legged, long-waisted number, lacking several inches of the six-foot mark but slender enough to seem taller. His double-breasted worsted suit was a soft shade of dark gray, his shirt a pale blue that narrowly missed being white. Where the wings of a soft collar met was a bow tie in white-and-blue faille that picked up the colors in a carelessly arranged display handkerchief.

You never can tell what's behind an outfit like that. He

could have just filed a bankruptcy petition or he might be carrying a gold-trimmed alligator wallet stuffed with thousand-dollar bills.

While he was getting into the customer's chair alongside the desk, I went back to open the window again. By the time I was ready to sit down, his topcoat was draped carelessly over his crossed legs and he was looking hard at me from above a not very faintly curled lip. When that had gone on long enough for me to learn who was running the interview, he said crisply, "I'm here only as a favor to a friend, Mr. Pine. Private detectives are out of my line and I can see I haven't missed much. So, if you don't mind, I'd like to get this over with quickly.

"I like your approach," I said. "In fact I'm crazy about it. Trot out your dirty linen and I'll have a look at it."

His face flamed. "There is no dirty linen, as you put it. I told you I'm acting for another party."

"Yeah. Then speak your piece or walk out the door. My time's not valuable but it's my own."

He swallowed it but the edges hurt all the way down. "Look here," he said stiffly. "There's no point in our being at each other's throats this way. It so happens you're causing a friend of mine no little worry and she's asked me to help straighten matters out."

He had my attention now—all of it. "This friend of yours—does she have a name?"

"I'm sure it will come as no surprise to you," he said coolly. "Her name is Rehak—Grace Rehak."

"What am I supposed to be doing that worries her?"

He lifted an eyebrow at me. "Oh, come now, Pine. Just for once forget this cagey routine. Yesterday Miss Rehak received a phone call telling her you were attempting to find her. Naturally she's interested in knowing why you're looking for her—as well as who hired you in the first place."

"Why, sure," I said airily. "I blab confidences at the drop of a hat. Can I lend you a hat to drop?"

He smiled without humor and laid an elbow on the edge of the desk and bent across it toward me. "Perhaps I could drop some money instead," he said softly. "Would that make a difference?"

"Money," I said, "is always pleasant. But it won't buy my immortal soul, as the man says. How much money did you have in mind?"

"Well . . . " His eyes roamed the office and whatever he was thinking of offering was revised sharply downward. "Let's say two hundred dollars."

"A nice round sum," I said. "You can get a man killed for as much—in some circles. And all you want for this fortune is the name of a client. An opportunity like this doesn't come along every day."

Color began to rise in the graceful column of his neck, but his voice stayed tightly under control. "Do we make a deal, Mr. Pine?"

I found a match and lighted a cigarette while he waited for his answer. "Before I help myself to your money I'll need some time to butter my conscience. Suppose I get in touch with you in a day or two?"

"That won't do," he said instantly. "It will have to be now."

I sighed. "Do tell. You drive a hard bargain, Mr.—— Do you have a name or do I call you X17?"

His thin nostrils flared. "You can call me Smith."

"Oh, yes. I've seen your name on a lot of hotel registers. Keep your king's ransom, Mr. Smith. If Miss Rehak wants information from me, she'll have to get it direct—in exchange for the information I want."

"She'll never agree to see you, Pine," he said firmly. "She's terribly frightened of blackmail. Grace has put her past behind her and made a new life for herself. If the . . . the people with whom she is now associated should learn of her life three years ago . . . well, it would kill her. That's why she's beside herself with worry right now over your efforts to find her. That's why she asked me to come to you."

"Your friend has nothing to be afraid of from me, Mr. Smith. If I was to go in for blackmail, I'd have a plush four-room office suite and patronize your tailor. Tell her that—and tell her I'll do business with her personally and in person, or not at all."

He chewed his lip and shook his head and rubbed out his cigarette and shook his head again. "I don't know, Pine," he muttered. "I don't see how . . . She's so . . . "

I said, "Does the name Laura Fremont mean anything to you?"

He sat very still, his eyes watching my face but seeming to go past it and on into a gray infinity. Presently he moistened his lips and said thoughtfully, "I'm afraid not. No. Is this Fremont person the one who hired you?"

"Just shooting the moon," I said carelessly.

He stood up and shook out the folds of his topcoat. "I'll tell her what you said, Pine. All I *can* do. Where do I call you—if it comes to that?"

"My number's in the book," I said. "If I'm not here you can leave a message with the clerk at my hotel. The Dinsmore Arms on Wayne Avenue."

He shook his head again, then eyed me narrowly as a new thought hit him. "I might be able to make it five hundred, Pine."

I said wearily, "Will you go out the door or out the window?"

He turned on his heel and left me, the topcoat trailing across one arm. I waited until the corridor door banged shut, then I got up and went quietly into the outer room and opened the door a crack and listened to the sound of short angry steps fade into silence. When I figured he had turned down the corridor to the elevators, I looked out, saw the dim length of hall was empty and went quickly along it in the opposite direction to the red globe marking the stairs.

At this hour only one of the two cages would be running. Being what it was, the Clawson Building didn't run to much traffic. If my luck was in, that one elevator would be on its slow and shaky way up in answer to Mr. Smith's ring.

Two floors below mine I came out into the hall and raced along it. I reached the double shafts just as the open grillwork began to vibrate. I jammed a thumb against the "up" button, heard a rasping buzz in the cage a floor below, and a moment later the car shuddered to a halt and the door slid back.

I already had a dollar bill out, rolled so the denomination didn't show. The man at the controls was young in years and new on the job: some apprentice the union had sent over to break in before trusting him with one of the modern jobs sported by the important buildings around town. His lumpy, not very smart face was wearing a bored expression under a too-large uniform cap. The bored expression changed to slack-jawed wonder when he saw me standing there, a finger to my lips and the other hand waving a greenback at him.

A finger to the lips meant nothing to him. "Going up," he said, several hundred decibles louder than necessary and gave me the jaundiced eye.

I stepped in quickly, slammed a hand down against the control lever and said softly, "Close that fat mouth of yours and listen. Get me to the first floor as fast as this pile of junk can make it."

The buzzer exploded into sound and the number 8 fluttered against a field of white on the automatic chart above the controls. The operator said, "I got a pickup on eight, mister. You wanta cost me—?"

My elbow in his ribs pried him away from the lever. Before he could get his breath back I shoved the handle in the right direction and the cage began to sink. He said, "Hey!" weakly and backed away, his eyes popping.

"This job may not mean much to you," I said. "But if you want to keep it, learn to humor the tenants." I pushed the bill into his hand. "If the passenger on eight wants to know why the delay, tell him the super got on and you had to run him down first. Got it?"

He nodded blankly and I let him have the controls in time to keep us out of the basement.

After the elevator started up again I went over and stood behind the door to the building stairs. When it came down a little later, Mr. Smith got out and went quickly to the street door and away. I slipped past the gawking operator and reached the street in time to see the slim back under the gray topcoat on its way east toward Michigan Avenue.

When he was half a block away, I got over to the curb and looked for a cab in the oncoming traffic. Not a one in sight; there wouldn't be. I began to walk east, keeping pedestrians between Mr. Smith and me, hoping he'd turn in at one of the shops or drop in somewhere for a drink: anything that would give me a chance to pick up transportation ahead of him.

It wasn't my day. A sleek black Cadillac sedan slid past me, rolled to the curb and a horn sounded a pleasant musical note. I caught a glimpse of black hair under a perky hat, the earpiece of a pair of sunglasses and the shoulder and sleeve of a gray-fur jacket.

And then the gray topcoat cut off my view, the car door

slammed shut, and the sedan floated on toward the avenue, made a graceful left turn there while the cop on duty gave the Fords and Chevvys the palm of his glove, and disappeared.

I got out a matchbook folder and started patting my pockets. One of these days I was going to start carrying a pencil. I stopped a paunchy bird in a green Homburg, borrowed his gold-plated fountain pen and wrote down the license number of the Cadillac sedan. A sudden gust of wind tried to get the folder before I could jam it back in my pocket.

Things were looking up. I had another lead now—a lead furnished by the obliging Mr. Smith. I was growing fond of Mr. Smith. Not the halfback type exactly, but a long way from drop-the-handkerchief. It was certainly kind of him to let me have this bright new lead. A lead to a girl I wasn't really looking for.

CHAPTER 9

THE day had become suddenly chill, almost cold in fact. A pale sun stood halfway down the western sky and a stiff breeze from the northwest was rising in the streets. Topcoat weather, a month ahead of time. It happens that way around Chicago in the early fall. Another twenty-four hours, even less, and you could be back in front of an electric fan.

At three-twenty I turned my car wheels out of the streetcar tracks on Broadway and drove slowly east along Surf Street. It was a street of residential hotels and court apartments, once fairly expensive, now well on the way downhill. Leaves scudded along the deserted walks and window awnings, and sidewalk canopies made harsh flapping sounds.

Number 470 proved to be a gray-stone double building of four floors. A signboard stuck in the left-hand section of a small ragged lawn mentioned that this was the Surfway Apartments, 1½-2-2½-3-room furnished apartments, Hoague & Pendelton agents, 131 West Washington Street, see janitor on premises. At the foot of the plate-glass door was an enameled plaque pointing out that all deliveries were to be made at the rear. It didn't say what would happen if you were caught sneaking in with a quart of milk.

I pushed into the hall. The floor was gray-and-white stone squares, a little dusty, some of them chipped at the edges. There were twin rows of mailboxes with bell buttons over the name plates and a locked inner door with finger smears on the glass. The lifeless air was laced with stale cigar smoke.

M. Conrad, according to one of the plates, occupied apartment 311. But not alone it seemed. Underneath the name was another. B. Field. No mention of G. Rehak there or on any of the others in either row. I wondered if Gracie had changed her name to Field.

While I was wondering about it, the inner door popped open and a stout middle-aged party with a red face under a dark-gray hat came through. He saw me standing there, jumped guiltily and scuttled past me and out before the pneumatic gadget on the inner door allowed it to close. I got to it in time to keep the lock from taking hold and looked back over my shoulder to the street door. The red-faced bird was nowhere in sight. I wasn't at all surprised. This was that kind of neighborhood.

I went on through into a dim narrow corridor with nobody around. Layers of quiet hung there with only the sounds of the wind from far off and the throb of a motor in the street. No elevator but there was a flight of carpeted steps leading upward. I climbed them to the third floor and followed my nose along a hall even dimmer than the one downstairs. Doors lined it, stained a light walnut, with numbers in pale ivory at eye level.

311 was nearly all the way back. No push button next to it so I knocked softly and felt the door move sluggishly under my knuckles. The lack of light had kept me from noticing it had already been open a crack. While I was wondering if that was important I knocked a second time.

No answer. Through the thin opening I could make out the shadowy outlines of a table with a wide-shaded lamp, the arm of a couch, a ribbon of dark rug. The only sound was the *plink . . . plink . . . plink* of water dripping against a drain.

She might have been sleeping. With the door open? Stranger things have happened. I leaned a hand against the door, swinging it still wider and said, "Miss Conrad?" Not loud but still strong enough to be heard. I put my head around the edge of the door and opened my mouth to call the name a second time.

I saw the shoes first, high-heeled black suede pumps propped up on their toes, a slim ankle in each. Dark nylons on slender legs, the edge of a skirt hiked up past the knees, the curve of hips. Along the back of my neck the short hairs lifted and stiffened. Or maybe I only imagined that.

A doorknob rattled somewhere down the hall. I stepped through and closed the door to 311 with my back. The wrong thing to do but there I was.

The body was face down, legs pointed toward me, one cheek against the rug and the other veiled by a cloud of dark hair. All I could make out in that light but it was more than enough. Another day, another corpse, another knot tightening under my ribs and filling my mouth with a metallic taste.

I crossed over to the lamp and turned it on. The room's grayness retreated to the corners. A living room, small, sparsely furnished with unimaginative stuff that was neither as tired nor as shabby as the neighborhood warranted. One window behind green draperies. Two doors, not counting the one to the hall. One was partly open, with the rhythmic drip of water sounding behind it; the other tightly closed, nearly touching the head of the girl on the floor.

I sniffed at the air. No smell of gunsmoke or rare Oriental poisons. I edged past the trim legs and knelt down and brushed the hair away from the cheek. It wasn't really dark hair after all, but a rich warm brown with what might have been a natural curl and a reddish glint from the light.

And she was breathing.

The knot under my ribs began to unravel. I put a finger against the artery in her firm young neck and felt the slow regular thump of her heart. No bruises that I could see. And no blood. Certainly no blood.

I got my arms under her and straightened up and carried her to the couch. She stirred slightly as I put her down. She moaned softly and the long curling eyelashes fluttered. She would be coming around any second now. It might have been only a faint, but she seemed too knocked out for that.

On the floor between the sofa and the closed door was a blue leather handbag. I stooped, picked it up and released the catch. The usual collection of junk, among it a checkbook in a black folder. I lifted the snap and saw a name and address printed in the lower left-hand corner of the top check. Susan Griswold, 1124 North Avon Road, Lake Ridge, Illinois. I knew about Lake Ridge, but only from hearsay. For upper-strata millionaires only. A municipality all to itself, located between Lake Forest and Highland Park along Lake Michigan fifteen miles north of the Chicago city limits. I leafed through the stubs to the last balance shown and whistled silently before letting the folder slip back into the bag.

While I was putting it down on the table, her eyes opened. They were gray-blue eyes, lovely eyes, quite large in a face that was on the small side. She didn't see me; it would be a moment or two before she saw anything. She groaned and put up a hand and touched one side of her head, high up, flinching under the slight pressure of her fingers. That answered one of my questions, but only one. I flinched a little with her, knowing how it would feel. I had been there myself—and recently.

When she started to push herself up in a fumbling way, I reached out to help her, propping her in a sitting position against one of the couch arms. Her head lolled to one side and the soft strands of hair moved across one eye. She brushed at it vaguely.

"My head hurts," she breathed. The words weren't for me. She didn't know I existed.

"Just let it go," I said. "These things take some getting over."

She blinked a time or two, getting me into focus. Her frown was more puzzled than anything else. "Are you the one who rescued me? Or have I been rescued?"

"All over by the time I showed up," I said. "My contribution was sweeping you off the rug."

She moved her hands aimlessly. They were small capable-looking hands that would handle a car or a tennis racket with casual competence. One of them was clenched into a loose fist. Something was in that fist, something that dangled its free ends against her wrist. Something that seemed to be a scrap of black lace.

She saw where I was looking and her own eyes dropped to the fist. Slowly she let the fingers peel back. It was lace all right—a ragged shred of it. Fragile and wispy, like the edging from a brassiere or a slip. I reached down and lifted it out of her unresisting hand.

I said, "What's been going on around here?"

She started to shake her head but thought better of it. "I'm not sure myself. I was supposed to meet Miss Conrad here at three o'clock. When she didn't answer my knock I thought she might not be awake yet. The door was unlocked, so I came on in and knocked on what I thought would be the bedroom door. I heard the creak of bed springs and then nothing at all. I knocked again and called out her name. She said to come in and I opened the door—and the roof caved in!"

"Why would she want to slug you?" I said.

"Good Lord, I don't know." She wet her lips. "You wouldn't happen to have a glass of water on you? I think there's a sand dune in my throat."

"Coming up," I said. I turned and went over to the partly open door and through it. Another small room, a kitchen this time, filled with ghostly half-light from a square window framed with a cottage curtain.

I found a glass on the porcelain sink and was reaching for the tap when I caught the faint click of metal against metal from the other room. I stepped back quickly and looked through the open doorway. Susan Griswold was at the hall door, a hand on the knob, ready to leave without saying good-by.

I was in there before she could get the door open more than a foot. I slapped a palm hard against the wood and the door banged shut. Our faces were no more than inches apart. Hers was flushed and the gray-blue eyes gleamed with anger and alarm. We stood like that, breathing at each other, not saying anything, while the seconds ticked away.

I said, "Thirst all gone, hunh?"

She didn't give an inch. I continued to look at her, really seeing her now. She was past twenty, but not very far past. She had all the figure any girl would want, no more and no less, wearing a gray-blue suit and a high-necked yellow sweater under that. The face had a wholesome out-of-doors look, with a dusting of cautious freckles across the bridge of a small nose. You wouldn't see the freckles until you were right on top of them. The mouth belonged to her type of face and suggested she would be generous to the people she liked. So far I didn't qualify. As a face it wouldn't start any wars but it would make coming home from one something special.

When she spoke there was an edge to her voice. "Look, I'm getting out of here."

"Not yet," I said. "Not until the clouds drift by. Let's go back and sit down. My feet hurt."

Her chin lifted. "Get out of my way."

I had a hand around her wrist before she knew it. She caught her breath and tried to jerk away. "Behave yourself," I growled and drew her away from the door. She hung back but it was no more than a token resistance.

She sank onto the sofa, rubbing her wrist where my fingers had been and stared at me sullenly. I found my cigarettes and shook one loose and held it out to her. She started to refuse, then shrugged and accepted it and a light. The set of her chin told me I might succeed in keeping her here but silence was all it would get me.

I left her there and prowled the room, looking for anything and nothing. The drip from the kitchen faucet went on and on, as wearing as any torture dreamed up by the Chinese.

When I reached what would be the bedroom I stopped. The knob turned easily under my hand and I jolted the door open with my knee. Not enough light to make out anything; if there was a window the blind was tightly drawn. The lamp behind me put a yellow oblong across the floor and halfway up the far wall. My shadow seemed all legs. A wall switch was just inside the door.

Pale-rose light sprang up from under frilly shades on a pair of vanity lamps. A full-sized bed with a low endboard. A chest of drawers between an open closet and the bathroom. Scatter rugs in white and brown to match the valance above a narrow window.

A clean, orderly, feminine room, with the smell of sandalwood lightly in the air and the smell of death even lighter but there just the same. Face up across the bed lay the body of a naked woman, a sun-tan stocking twisted tightly around her neck.

CHAPTER 10

SHE HAD died hard and not quick. The cream-colored spread was rumpled and half on the floor. Her coal-black hair was tangled. Her mouth was open wider than seemed possible and the tongue was enormous and the wrong color. Her eyes were swollen beyond their lids until they were no longer eyes but a nameless obscenity.

And for a final touch, four broad shallow scratches in leering red slanting across the white belly from below one over-ripe breast to a point well below the opposite ribs. Four parallel scratches, close together, left by four broad fingernails in one last gesture of contempt.

"Oh-h-h!" A soft stricken gasp from behind me. Susan Griswold was standing there, no blood in her face, her eyes dark with horror. I twisted sharply and closed the door hard, cutting us off from the bedroom. Her knees were buckling as I caught her. She leaned against me and began to shake.

I lugged her back to the couch and dumped her not gently on it. I sat down at the other end and lighted a cigarette and did nothing except breathe smoke for what seemed a long time. The wind, stronger now, whined uneasily past the window and in the kitchen the refrigerator clicked against the silence and began to hum quietly to itself.

And after a while I began to think again.

Susan Griswold's cigarette still smoldered, forgotten, between the ringless fingers of her left hand. I reached down and took it away and ground it out in a flat metal ash tray alongside the table lamp.

"You know who she is?" I asked.

She nodded and moved the tip of her tongue along her lips. "It's . . . Mary Conrad," she said, her voice barely audible.

"How well did you know her?"

"Not at all, really. I spoke to her twice, once on the phone."

"Any idea who would want her dead?"

"Of course not. How could I?"

"I thought I'd ask—although it's not my place to." I stood up slowly and looked around the room. "You say there's a phone here?"

Her expression was startled. "Phone? Why a phone?"

"To call the law," I said. "This is murder, lady. When a murder happens the cops have to know. I thought everybody knew that."

She jumped to her feet, ready to run. "I can't let them find me here. There isn't anything I can tell them anyway."

"That won't keep them from asking," I said. "Look, you were here, Miss Griswold. You got knocked on the head by the murderer. When you came to, there was a strip of lace in your hand—something you must have clawed from the killer while you were falling. That makes it a clue—and the police lab just loves clues. And they'll want to know why you were here to begin with."

She was rubbing a hand along the other wrist, over and over as if she was cold. "No!" The word came out loudly, driven by panic. "It's not so much what my being mixed up in a murder would do to my father. But if Eve found out I'd come here to see Mary Conrad . . . well, she'd guess what my reason was. That would put her on guard and I'd *never* find out anything."

"You're forgetting I missed the first act, Miss Griswold. Want to bring me up to date a little?" I asked.

It was a new thought to her. She looked at me narrowly, thinking about it. "What good would that do?" she said sharply. "I don't know you or anything about you."

I reached for my wallet. Her eyes jumped, following my hand. "No gun," I said solemnly, holding up the identification panel with the photostat of my business license in it.

She stared at it woodenly and from it to me. "A private detective," she said, almost groaning the words. "That's fine. That's simply wonderful. And all along I thought she didn't know. How much is she paying you to spy on me?"

"I'm very reasonable," I said. "Any housewife can afford me out of her pin money. No extra charge for insults."

"All right," she said, sighing. "I could be wrong and I hope I am. But you haven't said why you're here."

"Neither have you," I pointed out. "Me, I'm the guy who wants to yell for the cops—and intends to. Right now."

She caught my sleeve as I turned away. "I believe you! I have to believe you! Listen, Mr. Pine, if I tell you, if I convince you I couldn't possibly know who killed Mary Conrad, will you let me go? And not tell the police I was here?"

"You think I'm nuts?" I growled. "I could be crucified for a trick like that—and don't think they wouldn't enjoy doing it." I stuffed the wallet back in my pocket. "Tell it or don't tell it, Miss Griswold. But you'll get no guarantees."

She hesitated, covering it by sinking down on the couch again. She wanted desperately to come up with a quick convincing story that wouldn't expose her hand. But a lie that fast and smooth was beyond anyone of her background and tender years. And not with those eyes. They were as easy to read as the figures in her checkbook.

"Could I have another cigarette?" she said.

I took them out, lighted hers and one for myself, and sat down where I could see her face. I said, "Time figures in this, you know. It's okay to have somebody drop in and find us this way—after we notify the buttons."

She said, "I'm Susan Griswold, as you seem to have found out. Probably by going through my bag." She waited, for an apology most likely, didn't get one, bit her lip and went on. "My father is Lawrence Griswold. I suppose you know who he is."

"I don't think so. Not offhand."

"Well, for one thing, he's been married four times."

"That wouldn't even get him on page ten," I said. "Not these days."

"Must you be witty? I thought you said time was important."

"Carry on."

"My father married again six months ago," she said, not keeping the bitterness out of her voice and not trying to. "A tall leggy blonde like the last two before her. As beautiful on the outside as the angel he thinks she is. And behind all the glamor, even more grasping and selfish and—and deceitful than the others."

"You can see right through her, hunh?"

Her faced burned all the way to the hairline. "Listen, mister detective," she said through her teeth. "I don't think any more highly of daughters who try to break up second marriages than you do. But I've seen them come and go right past my nose. I've seen them marry my father for what they could pry out of him afterward. Just that and only that. Each one left him a little more disillusioned, a little more shaken, a little older in more than years."

"And don't forget the considerable loss to his bank account," I added.

"You think that means anything to me?" she blazed. "If that was as far as it went, I'd mind my own business. I certainly managed to the first couple of times. But not any more. This time he married a woman with brains—a woman who's not going to be satisfied with just kicking him in the teeth and taking a quiet divorce and a big settlement. This one's going after everything. Even if he has to die for her to get it!"

I said, "That's a nice round statement if I ever heard one. What have you got to back it up with?"

"Facts. Plus some things I can't put into words but are there just the same. For one, she's fired and replaced every servant we had—some of them with us for years. She hired a cold-blooded bitch—I'm sorry—of a personal secretary who'd stick a knife in her own throat if Eve told her to. And she's got some man, I mean my stepmother has, who's with her half the time, the kind of a person who looks like mineral oil tastes! Dad, of course, welcomes him right into the family. 'Any friend of my wife's is a friend of mine!' "

I said, "You've really convinced yourself."

Her small nostrils flared a little. "And you've already made up your mind that I'm strictly a jealous, meddlesome troublemaker who is determined to make my father unhappy. Is that it?"

"Probably not," I said. "Not if I'm to go by your stunning figure and your nice honest eyes. Does she know how you feel about her?"

"She knew it before I did," Susan Griswold said grimly.

"What was her name before she married your father?"

"Eve Shelby was her professional name. I don't know of any other."

"What was her profession?"

She fanned the smoke between us away with her hand.

"She sang at the Tropicabana. A night club and gambling spot out on the South Side. Dad married number three out of the same place. His one other weakness is roulette systems that never work and he spends two or three nights a week at the tables out there."

"It's a rocky road." I sighed. "Roulette and blondes. Sounds worse than a Georgia chain gang."

She bit down on her teeth and let that one go by. I put out my cigarette and lighted another without realizing it. "I get the background," I said, "but how does Mary Conrad fit in?"

Susan Griswold swallowed, remembering the corpse in the next room. "This is going to sound sort of silly, I suppose," she said uncomfortably. "But I had the feeling . . . no, it was more than that. I *knew* the time would come for a showdown between Eve Shelby and me. So I made up my mind to get all the—ammunition I could beforehand. Nobody seemed to know anything about her before she started singing at the Tropicabana—less than two months before she married Dad. I wondered about that. People cover up their past when they've got something to hide."

"True," I said. "How true. I find this fascinating, Miss Griswold. Only——"

"I'm coming to that," she said tartly. "You said to tell you and I'm doing it my way."

"Quite."

Her lips tightened but she went on, her voice clear and dry. "I learned one of the entertainers in the floor show at the Tropicabana had been a close friend of Eve's. Mary Conrad. I spoke to her at the club one night and let a hint drop that I'd be willing to pay well for information about Eve—the right kind of information. She said to give her a week to think it over, then to call her here at the apartment.

I telephoned about one o'clock this afternoon and we made a date for three."

I shook my head. "It wasn't smart, Miss Griswold."

"What wasn't smart?"

"Going to the Conrad dame that way. Odds are strong she went straight to your stepmother with the whole story."

"Then why see me today?"

"Maybe to give you some facts. The kind of facts Mrs. Griswold would want you to have. Did Mary Conrad let out anything at all over the phone or that first time at the night club?"

She gnawed at her lower lip, thinking. "No . . . just that she roomed with Eve about two years ago."

The cigarette fell out of my hand. I bent slowly and picked it up and blinked at it. Susan Griswold was staring at me, her lips slightly parted, a wrinkle in the clear skin above her eyebrows.

"You don't say." My voice sounded hoarse and I cleared it. "You mean . . . right here?"

"*What* right here?"

"Did Mary Conrad room with Eve Shelby at *this* address?"

"Well, I don't know *that*. She didn't say and I didn't ask her. Is it important?"

"One never knows," I said vaguely. I fingered ash into the tray and studied the nice frank lines of her lovely face. "And this," I said, "all this you've told me so you could walk out of here before the sirens start screaming. This proves you can't furnish any leads to who tied a knot in Mary Conrad's windpipe. Have you actually missed the entire point or are you waiting for me to put it into words for you?"

"If you're going to be clever," she said impatiently, "don't take so long at it. What point have I missed?"

"Let's take it step by step," I said. "You came up here at

three o'clock to get information from Mary Conrad. She knew you were coming and she knew the time you'd arrive. You came up, found the door open and started into the bedroom and somebody laid you out."

"But I don't know who it was," she said quickly.

"But it was a woman," I said. I brought the strip of lace out of my pocket and held it in front of her eyes. "She clouted you and you fell down. But not before you grabbed at her and got part of her underwear. How does that sound?"

Her eyes flickered. "Yes," she breathed. "I remember now. She hit me and I started to fall. I threw out my hands and caught hold of her. Something tore and she hit me again. That's all I remember."

"That should be plenty. Find the woman who wanted Mary Conrad killed and the mystery is solved. And even without seeing this woman, we know a thing or two about her."

I had thrown her again. "I don't see how——"

"Well, Mary Conrad was no vest-pocket edition," I said. "You saw that yourself. It takes a good-sized woman to overpower and strangle anybody—even another woman."

"Well, ye-e-s," she admitted, dragging out the second word. "But that still——"

"Maybe I got the wrong picture," I said. "But from the way you described Eve Griswold I assume she's not exactly an invalid."

Her jaw dropped so hard it almost bounced. "Are you suggesting Eve could have—?"

"Why not, Miss Griswold? Look at it a little. What if she got to worrying that Mary Conrad might let the wrong thing slip? Your stepmother could have found out what time you were coming here today. She could have arrived shortly ahead of you, done the job and left you on the floor to take the rap. I'm just using your own analysis of her."

She liked it. She liked it fine. The light gleamed along her eyes and a small smile was on its way to being born. And then the smile died there and her eyes seemed to film over.

"No." Her small firm breasts, pushing against the yellow sweater, rose and sank as she sighed. "No. I simply don't believe it."

"Why not?" I said. "Because you've changed your mind about what she's capable of, or because having her arrested on suspicion of murder would be a haymaker to your father? Look, you want to get rid of her, don't you? Legally?"

"Y-you're only guessing. Others could have wanted Mary Conrad killed. I don't know a thing about her. Do you?"

"The police will run down any leads furnished them, Miss Griswold. I'm not saying they'll slap your stepmother in the chair tomorrow. But you can see that she might have done in Mary Conrad. Why not let them work on that angle?"

She said coldly, "Why are you so anxious to get her involved in this? What difference does it make to you?"

"Just trying out for the Boy Scouts." I yawned and continued to sit there, moving the fragment of lace around in my fingers. Cheap stuff, I decided, not handmade, not at all what you'd expect to find next to the skin of an angel accustomed to wallowing in earthly luxury. I put it to my nose and sniffed and drew a blank. No "My Sin" or "Temptation" or "Prétexte." Whoever it had belonged to might touch up the tips of her ears now and then but she kept the stuff out of the valley.

I said, "How did you get in downstairs?"

"Get in?" she said blankly.

"Past the inner door," I said impatiently. "Did you ring the bell or use a key or knock it in with a fire ax?"

"Oh—that!" Her expression cleared. "The janitor—I suppose that's who he was—was sweeping the hall and the door was propped open. Since I knew her apartment number and was expected anyway, I didn't bother to ring the bell."

"I was afraid of something like that," I said. "Did he get a good look at you?"

"Not that I noticed. He didn't even turn his head."

"He must be an old man. Nobody saw you on your way into the apartment?"

"Frankly I wasn't paying much attention. But *I* didn't see anybody, if that's any help."

"Which leaves only the janitor," I mused. "And since this is a big building with a lot of apartments, he would see too many people to remember any certain one."

"I suppose," she observed dryly, "that this is all terribly important."

"It is to you," I said. "It leaves the chances of somebody tipping off the bulls about you very remote."

Sudden hope lighted up her face. "Then you don't intend to hold me for the police? Is that what you're saying?"

I spread my hands. "Holding people is a cop's job. As a law-abiding citizen it's my duty to detain, whenever possible, any person observed in the act of committing a felony. I haven't observed you committing anything, Miss Griswold."

She was on her feet and two steps from the couch before a sudden thought stopped her and turned her around. "Why the change of heart?" she demanded suspiciously. "You made this sound altogether different only a few minutes ago."

"You ever hear about gift horses, Miss Griswold? Maybe I'll need a favor from you someday. To earn it, I'm letting you breeze on out, hoping of course that I won't get backed into a corner where I'll have to tell the homicide boys about you."

Her eyes narrowed until they were slits. "What favor do you have in mind?"

I grunted. "Maybe a yacht, maybe your pure white body, maybe only a kind word." I stood up and stretched. "If you're not leaving, you might as well help me find where the phone's hidden."

While I was halfway to the bedroom I heard the hall door close softly behind her.

CHAPTER 11

I WAS in the bathroom unscrewing the top from an aspirin bottle when the downstairs buzzer went off. My hand jerked, knocking a toothbrush behind the toilet bowl. I carried the aspirin bottle into the living room without realizing it and pushed the button.

Two uniformed prowl-car men came hurrying along the hall, panting a little, watching the numbers. When they saw me standing in the doorway to 311, they galloped over and combed me with their eyes.

The taller of the pair said tonelessly, "All right, buddy. Inside."

They rode me in and closed the door and I got looked at some more in the impersonally tough way a cop looks at everything including his watch. Both were big men, with the flat unrelaxed faces issued to all members of any police force along with their badges. They could have driven trucks or built your house or owned the corner grocery. One had blue eyes, one had brown; one had a long thin nose, the other a blob of shapeless flesh to breathe through; one was fifty if a day, the other was stepping into thirty-five. Yet their uniforms and their expressions made them twins.

Their eyes went quickly around the room, missing nothing. They looked at me, at my face, at my general build, at the aspirin bottle in my hand. The younger let his right hand drift down until it rested on the flap of a black leather holster at his hip.

"Your name Pine?"

I said my name was Pine.

"Where's this stiff?"

I flapped a hand at the closed door to the bedroom. The cop looked at the door and back to me. He turned the stud on his holster flap and got out the heavy black gun. He did it with swift ease, like the sheriff of Tombstone.

"Turn around and get them hands up," he said, tough in a polite way. Or it might have been polite in a tough way.

I turned lazily, holding both hands at shoulder level, one still clutching the aspirin bottle but not intending to hit anybody with it. The same old routine as in every crime-fighter movie. Only the movies hadn't originated it.

A hand patted me here and there from behind, as business-like and detached as a tailor at work. It hit the bulge under my left arm, froze briefly, then darted under my lapel and came out with my gun. The gun disappeared and I heard a sniffing sound that meant he had his beak buried in the muzzle. I drew down my hands without being told and turned slowly.

The cylinder was turned out and he was counting bullets. The chambers were filled except for the one the hammer rested against. He gave me a thin, up-from-under glare, clicked the cylinder shut with a sharp movement of his hand and dropped the gun into one of the roomy side pockets of his uniform coat.

"This makes it tough on you, buddy," he growled. "Concealed weapons is against the law."

"Should have ditched it, huh? Before I called homicide."

That hadn't occurred to him. Either I hadn't been smart or there was more to me than met the eye. "Let's see your identification."

I hauled out my wallet and he leafed through it. When I

got it back there was no more mention of the gun but it stayed in his pocket. He kept his eye on me while I retreated to the couch, then shifted his gaze to his partner.

"Take a look in there, Frank."

Frank stalked over to the bedroom door, opened it and went in. The young cop slid his gun into its holster and stayed where he was, flexing the fingers of his right hand over and over. In the silence I heard the wind still going nowhere fast and loud. The cop and I were watching each other like a couple of strange dogs that could get to be friends if first appearances held up, when Frank ambled out of the bedroom.

"Dame, all right," he said. He winked heavily and grinned a dirty grin. "A looker and nood as they come. Silk stockin' around her neck."

The young cop wet his lips uncertainly. He wanted to go in and get an eyeful but was reluctant to appear obvious about it. While he was thinking up the right words to justify doing so, the first-floor buzzer gave a Bronx cheer and he went over and tried to shove the release button through the wall. I leaned back and found a cigarette and lighted it. All traces of Susan Griswold's red-tipped cigarettes were gone from the ash tray. The table lamp and the doorknobs had only my prints on them. The unknown killer would have been smart enough not to leave any.

The prowl-car men drifted aimlessly about the room until the door pushed all the way open and three officers in plain clothes stalked in. The young uniform cop saluted awkwardly and tilted his head at me. "This guy found her, Captain. Woman's on the bed in there."

I was looked at briefly and without warmth, then the three of them entered the bedroom. Almost immediately the buzzer sounded again and the young cop admitted four men from the crime laboratory judging from the bags and cameras they carried. They joined the detectives and we had a spell of quiet and after a while the captain came out again.

He was a tall man, not as wide as a two-car garage and no fat on him. His face was bony, broad across the cheeks and pointed at the chin. Thin lips framed a large mouth and he had wide-set yellow-green eyes below heavy brows. He was old enough to have gray hair which receded off a high rounded forehead. A lightweight gray hat was pushed far back on his head, its black ribbon faded out from many cleanings. His brown suit had a fine dubonnet stripe, hardly noticeable, and needed pressing although it was clean and fitted him right.

He said something under his breath to one of the cops, didn't wait for an answer and came over and nodded briefly to me, not tough and not gentle. "I'm Captain Blauvelt—Sheffield Avenue Station." Nothing distinctive about his voice. "How much am I going to get out of you?"

"All there is to get," I said. "I'm afraid it won't be much."

"Well now, I'm sorry to hear that. But even a little might turn out to be enough. They tell me you're a private star. I hope you're not one of the smart-aleck kind."

He could be a fool or it could be his way of talking. I leaned toward the second theory. I put on my bland expression and said nothing. He swiveled his eyes around the room until he saw the open door to the kitchen and the light coming through it from the overhead fixture I had switched on before the two cops arrived. "Let's have us a talk in there," he said.

"One thing, Captain," I said, getting up. "I'd like my gun back. One of the patrolmen is holding it for me."

He looked at me narrowly, then over to the boys in blue. "I'll take the gun," he said. "Better get back to your car and check in with Abrams."

The young cop, keeping his feelings off his face, brought

out my Detective Special and laid it in the center of Blauvelt's flat, long-fingered hand. There was a heavy plain gold ring on one of the fingers.

Still holding the gun he turned and walked into the kitchen, and I tagged along. He sat down at the white enameled table and pointed to the remaining chair. He took off his hat and mopped his forehead and neck with a white handkerchief from a back pocket. When he reached for it I saw the butt of a heavy gun in an arm holster. He put away the handkerchief and sat there dancing my gun lightly on his hand and looking at me intently.

"So far," he said suddenly, "I got nothing but your word you're a private dick. Prove it to me."

Once more I dug out my wallet and placed the photostat and a business card on the table in front of him. He spent enough time on the first to memorize it, then fingered the card, his expression telling me what he thought of such fripperies. "What else?"

"That leaves the telephone," I said. "Ike Crandall, with the State's Attorney, knows me but he won't brag about it. Or Lieutenant Overmire, Central Homicide. He's not crazy about me either, but he'll tell you I'm not wanted for anything. I can give you the names of a lawyer or two, but not unless you insist."

"Sounds okay," he said grudgingly while I reloaded my wallet and got rid of it. "I'm not spending an hour checking them people—not over a Surf Street floozie. Or is that all she is?"

"Search me, Captain."

He patted the table's porcelain surface and sighed. "Christ, I'm dry. Hell of a wind coming up."

I left the chair and went over to the refrigerator. There were four bottles of beer, two quarts of milk with the cream poured off one, some sliced tomatoes on a cracked plate, the ruins of a pork roast. I said, "Beer or milk, Captain?"

"Milk? Don't tell me that floozie had kids!"

"Grownups have been known to drink the stuff. Beer, hunh?"

"If she's cold."

I took out two of the bottles and removed the caps with an opener hanging above the sink. The cupboard yielded two tall glasses. Blauvelt put my gun on the table and poured for both of us and we watched the foam settle. He emptied the glass in four gulps and pushed it back along the table and shook his head when I reached for the bottle.

He let out his breath and closed his eyes and opened them again. "Who is she, Pine?"

"Mary Conrad. With the floor show at the Tropicabana, a nightspot on East Fifty-third."

"I know where it is. Who shoved her?"

"By me, Captain."

"Dead when you found her, eh?"

"I'd hate to have you think different."

"Girl friend of yours?"

"Nothing like that. I never saw her alive. This was a matter of business."

"Tell me about it."

I hunched my shoulders and put my elbows on the table. "I was hired to find a girl—the daughter of an elderly couple from out of town. She'd come to Chicago a couple of years ago and dropped out of sight. Mary Conrad, it seems, had roomed with her for a short time right after she arrived in town. I learned Conrad's address and came around to see what she could tell me. I was a little too late."

"How could you get in if she was already dead?"

"Well, the downstairs door was open and I didn't bother

to ring. When I got up here the apartment door was ajar and knocking didn't bring any answer. I wondered why anybody would go away and leave the door open, so I kind of looked the place over."

He made a small noise deep in his throat that might have meant almost anything. "That's all, Pine?" he asked silkily.

"All except my phone call to the bureau."

"Uh-hunh. You sure glossed this one over, brother. What I mean! Doors all open for you, body waiting, killer gone. And that's all." He tilted back on his chair, steadying himself with a hand against the table edge, and rubbed a forefinger thoughtfully against the hinge of his sloping jaw. "Well, it could of happened; I don't say no. But you left out a hatful. What's about this dame you're supposed to find? What name?"

"Laura Fremont," I told him reluctantly.

"From out of town, you said. Whereabouts out of town?"

"Nebraska."

"You hired by letter or something?"

"It started that way. I drove out there and talked to her folks."

"They give you this lead on Conrad?"

"Nothing for you down that street, Captain. The Fremonts didn't have the name of any of Laura's Chicago friends."

"Dug it up yourself, hunh? What other leads you got?"

"This was the first," I said bitterly. "I hope the others turn out different."

He lowered the chair legs back to the floor, dug under his coat and brought out a cigar with a gaudy band and a mottling of unripened leaves running through it. Not a Corona—not by a long way. He bit off the end and spat it on the floor and used one of my matches to light what was left. It smelled like a plumber's candle. In the silence I could hear men moving around in the other rooms and the murmur of voices.

"That wind's sure a bitch," Blauvelt said conversationally. "Listen to her! Like to blown us into a streetcar on the way over." The match followed the cigar tip to the floor. "Quite a broad, that Conrad. You get a good look at her?"

"I kept from drooling, if that's what you're after," I said harshly.

"Kind of cute in a filled-out way," he observed, smirking. "Man's going to look at a naked woman no matter she's dead or not. Real nice skin and stacked pretty too. She must've drove the boys wild—but she's worm food now. You got here when?"

"Three-thirty or a little after."

"She got it before three is my guess," he went on dreamily. "Doc might change that but not by much. Let's see your hands."

I had expected that. I put them, palms up, on the table in front of him. He took a pencil flash from a vest pocket and gave my nails a going over. He sighed finally and clipped the flash next to his fountain pen and leaned back to puff on his cigar.

"Didn't make you for a Ripper," he admitted. "Not that that would keep me from looking. Not even a little honest dirt under them."

Before I could answer that the way it deserved to be answered, one of the plain-clothes men strolled into the kitchen. He was a thin-faced, bored-looking number, with a pair of heavy-lidded eyes that would miss seeing anything smaller than the virus of the common cold. He drooped against the refrigerator door and said carelessly, "We uncovered a little something, Captain."

"Don't mind Mr. Pine here, sergeant," Blauvelt said with exaggerated politeness. "You might say he's working our side of the street. Trot her out, Les."

Les straightened long enough to bring up a cupped hand and reverse it above the table. A torn segment of black lace floated down to land lightly between Blauvelt and me. "Laying right under one of her hands," Les drawled. "Nothing we could find that it come off of. Renaldi thinks it's the trimming on a slip or a brassiere."

My face ached from my effort to keep it relaxed. Blauvelt reached out, felt the material, sniffed at it, let it drop back on the table. "Well, well," he said brightly, almost too brightly. "That kind of makes another woman the killer. Conrad puts up a fight, say, and tears the other dame's clothes some." He poked a long forefinger thoughtfully at the lace. "Only I'd like it a lot better had you pried this out of her hand, 'stead of finding it laying around loose. What else you got, Les?"

The other man's loose features twisted into a smirk. "Starts getting on the crummy side, Chief. Turns out this Conrad babe was a Lesbo. Queer as a set of purple teeth."

That jarred me all the way down to my socks. And of course both cops would be watching me. I reached for a cigarette and made a production of lighting it, getting my indifferent look back again.

"Well now," Blauvelt purred. "So she wasn't for the boys after all. Seems a pity, don't it?" He scratched the base of his thumb and blinked his yellow-green eyes like an oversize tiger digesting a native. "Who put you on to that, Les?"

"I checked with the boys downtown on a hunch," Les admitted smugly. "It showed on her record—what little record there was. Probation on a shoplifting charge, and a nolpross on a con-game beef. But she's been tied in with a bunch of Lesbos for years."

Blauvelt clucked his tongue and looked at me through the smoke screen I was building. "How much of this means something to you, Pine?"

"None of it."

"This girl you was hired to find—she one of them, too?"

"I started working on this job only a few hours ago, Captain."

"Now you know that ain't what I asked you," he said reproachfully.

"It still answers your question," I said. "The girl is missing and that's all I can tell you about her."

"Well now, this lets you know a little more and you're welcome to it. But you did say she used to room with Mary Conrad. So now it turns out Conrad was queer. Kind of seems likely this here Fremont girl is that way too, wouldn't you think?"

I didn't say anything. I was remembering what Mrs. Fremont had said about her daughter's attitude toward the male population of Lincoln. There were other things the old lady had said, and I was bringing them out and making a pattern of them. I began to feel on the sick side.

Captain Blauvelt sucked at a tooth and watched me over his cigar. "Not much question about it any more that a woman pushed Conrad. Not after hearing this. Still going to hunt up Laura Fremont, Pine?"

"I don't see why not. I was hired to find her."

"You private stars get tangled into some mighty smelly cases, I guess."

I shrugged and said nothing.

"Bring her around to see me, Pine. When you locate her."

"*If* I locate her," I said. "And you're taking a hell of a lot for granted if you try to tie her in with this killing. As I heard it, Mary Conrad was mixed up with a number of Lesbians. Any one of them might have strangled her in a jealous rage. Why single out someone for the job who knew her for only a short time—and that all of two years ago?"

The captain looked at Les and Les looked back at the captain. Blauvelt picked up his bottle and emptied the rest of the beer into his glass and drank it down. He sat there holding the glass and watching me burn.

"We'll need your prints," he said finally. "For elimination purposes, you understand. One of the boys will take them on your way out."

"Yeah," I said. "Then I'm not riding over to the station?"

"Not on a piddling little murder like this one. Drink your beer."

"No, thanks." I flipped my cigarette into the sink. "No more questions?"

"Guess not. Why don't you go home?"

"I had thought of it," I said. "How about my gun?"

He looked at the short and deadly length of it there on the table at his elbow. He pushed it delicately along the porcelain toward me, using his thumbnail. "Your gun don't interest me, pal. She was knocked off with a silk stocking. Pick it up."

"Nylon," I said. "You hardly ever see silk these days."

He leered again. "Not much you didn't take a good look!"

I put the gun away and the three of us walked into the living room. The prowl-car men were gone but the lab crew was still hard at work. One of them did a fast job of taking my fingerprints and handed me some gasoline on a cloth to clean away the excess ink. When I left, Captain Blauvelt was still wearing a trace of his leer.

I came very close to telling him what he could do with it.

CHAPTER 12

LaSalle Street, in the sixteen hundred block, was part of a lost neighborhood taken over largely by lost people. Up and down its length were cut-rate liquor stores, dingy restaurants with hectographed bills of fare stuck in fly-specked windows, and dirty-fingered little stores where a bell rang when the street door opened. But mostly there were cheap apartment buildings and seedy hotels with high-toned names and rooming houses that catered to old men with nothing left but limp pensions.

I parked the car around a corner and came back through the wind, a driving gale now, to 1682. It had been a private residence once upon a time: two floors of frame construction set back from the sidewalk, with a wide veranda, a gabled roof, dormer windows and a gingerbread trim—all of it painted an unlovely green too many years before.

I climbed three wooden steps to the porch and looked at a sun-yellowed Apartments card behind the glass of a bay window. Farther along the porch a cane-bottomed rocker jiggled in the wind. It didn't appear to have been sat in recently.

There were no bell buttons in sight and only a rusty hinge where once had been a knocker. I pushed open the street door and entered the cool funereal silence of a dim hall with wallpaper the color of mildew and tobacco-colored carpeting underfoot. Two doors, closed, were in the left wall and across the way a set of double rollback doors where once had been the dining room and might still be for all I knew. A bow-legged table against one wall held a few pieces of mail strewed along its surface.

No sign of life. No sound except the whine of wind and the muted slither of traffic. Nothing but a smell that was an accumulation of smells. And in the middle of it all, one lean corpse-weary private detective earning his daily bread.

I knocked on the blotched varnish covering one of the single doors.

Springs creaked, heels hit the floor, a throat was cleared, the door opened about a foot.

In years he was no more than nineteen, wearing unpressed trousers and a not very white shirt open at the collar and two buttons missing. A limp cigarette hung from the corner of a crooked mouth filled with petty meanness. He had thick black hair that had been slept in, narrow eyes loaded with suspicion, cunning and distilled hate, a thin tubercular face the color of boiled pork.

He said, "What'll it be, Jack?" in a voice built for profanity.

I said, "Miss Fremont."

He blew out some smoke without removing his cigarette. The smoke went into my face. That made no difference to him. "No one here by that name."

"I'll talk to the manager," I said.

"No manager. My old lady owns the joint. What d'ya want?"

"Call her. She might let you listen."

I was looked at, up and down, with a curled lip added for ballast. "Don't let's crack wise, Jack. I don't owe ya nothin'."

"No wonder the vacancy card's in the window," I said. "A doorman like you could be quite a liability."

His gray face turned a mottled pink. It was no improvement. I slid my foot ahead just as he heaved against the door. It hit and snapped back, catching him on the shoulder. The cigarette fell out of his face, striking the doorknob and giving off a shower of sparks.

His eyes were hot as a cobra's breath. I leaned on my side of the door and grinned at him. "Let's not wear out the act, Junior. I want a word with the right party and I'll be here until then. Believe me."

From somewhere behind him a door opened and shut and slippers flapped along the floor. A woman's voice, high and stagy, said, "To whom are you speaking, Gilbert dear?"

Gilbert muttered the word I had expected all along and retreated a few steps. My foot absently nudged the door, swinging it open, letting me see most of the room and the woman in it.

She was a tall number, lean as the toprail of a backwoods fence. Her hair had run the gantlet of dyes until it was now no color at all and she wore it in stiff waves worse than outright disorder. She had a collection of sharp-edged features in a puffy gray sliver of face balanced on a thin neck filled with stringy muscles. A quilted green bathrobe was wrapped around her, with a once pink nightgown trailing to mules with white pompons and runover heels.

She stood with her head tilted back, looking at me along a pointed nose like Catherine the Great inspecting a peasant from the wrong side of the Urals. Her smile was an impersonal thing, although she was trying to make it worth a duel in the gray dawn.

She said, "How *do* you do? I am Cornelia Van Cleve. Was there something?"

She treated the letter R like a vaudeville Englishman with a cold. I clawed off my hat and moved it around in my hands. "Good afternoon, Mrs. Van Cleve. I was inquiring about Laura Fremont."

"I'm afraid there's no one here by that name."

"I know," I said. "She moved out some months ago. Her folks haven't heard from her since and are starting to worry." I looked past her and smiled my dimpled smile. "I could come in and tell you about it."

She brought up a hand slowly, light glinting on flaking red nail polish, and touched the hair at the base of her neck. Some women can knock your eye out with that gesture. But not this woman. "I'm afraid the apartment isn't very tidy, Mr.——"

"Pine," I said. "I know how it is. I didn't get a chance at the breakfast dishes myself."

Gilbert was still in my way, glaring at me. I started in, forcing him to move or get stepped on. He turned in a tight circle and stalked over and dropped on a metal day bed along one wall. It held a tangle of gray sheet and thin blue blanket.

Mrs. Van Cleve closed the door and suggested I might find the couch just the thing for sitting purposes. I picked my way through a collection of mismatched and unattractive furniture coated with generations of dust and soft-coal smoke until I reached the couch. It had a coarse brown tapestry cover and loose springs in the wrong places but was probably more comfortable than the floor.

She sat down across from me, arranging the robe and nightgown to show me a scaly length of shinbone. Her smile was as sharp as the prow of a cruiser and about the same shape. Above and behind her a sick-looking canary moved sluggishly in a dull brass cage on a tall thin brass pole. The room smelled of old vegetable dinners. I scratched my knee.

She was still playing lady of the manor but her expression said she'd be willing to take time out for a little backstairs gossip. "Laura Fremont, did you say? I've had this place for seven years, Mr.—Pine, I believe you said?—and there's been no girl here by that name. I'm *so* sorry."

In the dusty silence a spring creaked in the day bed across the room where Gilbert sat with his back propped against the wall. I tapped my fingers gently on the sofa arm and tried to see past the sharp features and bored-duchess expression on the woman across from me. There seemed no reason for her to lie to me, but the reason could be there just the same.

"Think back a little," I said doggedly. "Tall for a girl, light-brown hair, a hundred and forty pounds. Blue eyes and more than likely pretty. But not a clinging vine. Moved out last January. Maybe she had her own apartment; maybe she shared it. Might even have had a little trouble over the rent or something—although I'm only guessing on that."

More silence. But this time it was silence filled with electricity. Mrs. Van Cleve's hands lifted, jittered, fell back in her lap. Anger struggled with fear in her eyes and in pinched lines about her thin beak of a nose. Her mouth opened and closed twice before anything came out of it.

"Why—why—you must mean that horrible, *horrible* Fairchild woman!" she moaned. "It was in January that ——"

Gilbert's heels hit the floor hard and he was off the day bed. One of his feet struck something a glancing blow, sending it skittering along the carpet. He took three fast steps that brought him to the center of the room. His face was red now and filled with bitter fury.

"Copper!" he spat. "Just one more wise flatfoot tryin' out a cute new twist! You guys don't ever let nothin' lay, do ya?"

I saw what it was his foot had hit against. A dime-store plate, crusted with stains of blueberry pie. I didn't see the fork anywhere. Maybe he had eaten it along with the pie.

I looked from the plate to Gilbert and back to the woman

again. She was sitting as stiff as a cement pretzel, her mouth still open but no words coming out.

It seemed my turn to say something. "The Fairchild woman is the one I had in mind, Mrs. Van Cleve. How do I get in touch with her?"

Her jaw snapped shut and her eyes got a little wild. Gilbert brought up a hand suddenly and rubbed the palm hard against his shirt front. "A big laugh!" Still loud, still filled with windy anger, but underneath the loudness and the anger was a whining note. "Whyn't you monkeys lay off, for Chrisake? Okay, so she got a sock wrapped around her neck and you guys took her out and buried her someplace. We told the captain what we could and that shoulda ended it. What else d'ya want?"

There was a cigarette in my mouth and I was through lighting it before I knew what my hands were doing. I scowled at the match and blew it out and bent what was left of the stick. I got up to take a Chinese-red ash tray off a table and carried it back to the couch. They watched me without moving and without a word.

I said, "Tell me the story, Mrs. Van Cleve. Once more and all of it."

Gilbert was still in the way. "The story ain't changed none, copper. Just kind of shove the hell off, hunh?"

I looked at him the way a homicide cop looks at people who get underfoot. "We never did write you off on this caper, Junior. Now I see why."

He made a strangled sound and his right hand balled into a fist and came down hard against the side of his thigh. I kept on looking at him. He turned sharply and went back to the day bed. He kicked the pie-stained plate clear across the room on the way. It hit the baseboard beside the door and spun like a coin and fell over.

Mrs. Van Cleve hadn't so much as turned her head while this was going on. I blew out some smoke and crossed my legs and said, "You were going to tell me about it, madam. As I understand it, you found the body."

"It was horrible!" she said suddenly. "I never did trust that Louise. Ellen was so quiet and polite, while the Fairchild woman never had anything to say. Just sneaked around with that better-than-anybody expression and her nose in the air. And then one night she choked Ellen to death with a stocking and went out and never came back!"

"Louise Fairchild did the job? You're sure of that?"

"Why, of course!" The question startled her. "She never came back, did she?"

"What was Ellen's last name?"

"Purcell. I told the captain all about——"

"And when did this happen?"

"In the night sometime. I told the captain——"

"I meant the date, Mrs. Van Cleve."

"The—? Oh, the *date!* January the something. Sixteenth? A Sunday. I'm sure it was the sixteenth, because Edna's birthday—Edna's my sister—her birthday was exactly one week later."

You sat and listened or you stood and listened. And when the calluses got thick enough so you didn't fidget, then you could be a private detective.

She went on babbling but I had stopped listening and started thinking. Seven times out of ten the alias starts with the same initials as the real name. That helps them remember and explains the initials on the suitcases and the handkerchiefs. Louise Fairchild. Laura Fremont.

I ground out my cigarette and stood up and went over to the bird cage. The canary sat on its perch and looked sullenly at me out of beady eyes. It probably didn't like cops either. I returned to the couch and sat down on a different broken spring and inspected the life line in my right palm. It wasn't a very long line and that cheered me a little.

I said, "The description I gave you a moment ago—does it fit Louise Fairchild?"

"Yes, sir." She fumbled a handkerchief from the torn pocket of her robe and dabbed at the corners of her eyes. It wasn't a very clean handkerchief and her eyes were as dry as Carrie Nation's cellar. "That's exactly the way I told the captain she looked. Although I must say he didn't seem very interested."

That failed to surprise me. The police didn't make a practice of working too hard on obscure killings in LaSalle Street kitchenettes. If they happened to pick up the guilty party with the knife in her hand and blood on her sleeve and the urge to sign a forty-page confession, that was one thing. But when it meant a lot of hard work running down blind leads, then the file would drift into the unsolved drawer to collect the dust of disinterest.

"Tell me what you can about both girls, Mrs. Van Cleve," I said.

"I really don't know a thing about them, Mr. Pine."

"Oh, cut it!" I snapped in my best servant-of-the-people tone. "Those two girls lived here for months and you couldn't help picking up something we can use. Where they worked, who they bought their groceries from, who their boy friends were. This is murder, madam, and you'll either give us a little co-operation or we'll get it another way. Just make up your mind which it's to be."

It didn't scare her into crawling under a chair but it did melt down what was left of her House of Hapsburg pose and start her talking. Skimmed down, it revealed that they were strange girls who kept to themselves and said little to

Mrs. Van Cleve and nothing to the other tenants. No boy friends ever called on them, although two girls, no description furnished, came to visit them a few times. Miss Fairchild worked days and the Purcell girl worked nights, although just where they worked Mrs. Van Cleve had no idea.

"The check!" she said suddenly.

I leaned back and groped for a cigarette. I said, "The check. Tell me about the check, Mrs. Van Cleve."

"It was from a night club. I remember now! With a long name. I remember thinking it was such a strange name."

It couldn't have been any except one. The name came automatically to my lips. "The Tropicabana?"

"That's it! That's the one!" She sounded pleased and proud of herself. "A pay check, it was. I could tell because they took out for Social Security and so on. And they used a check-writing machine. I distinctly remember! She paid the rent with it. The only time it wasn't in cash."

"Which of the two girls gave you the check, Mrs. Van Cleve?"

"The one that worked nights. Ellen—Ellen Purcell. The poor unfor——"

"Why didn't you tell the captain about this, madam?"

"Didn't even *think* of it! If you hadn't kept asking me . . ."

I rolled the cigarette thoughtfully around in my fingers. "So Louise Fairchild murdered Ellen Purcell, then quietly packed up and eased out of the picture. That's the last you heard of her?"

"Well, she didn't take any luggage. Left everything upstairs."

"What happened to the stuff?"

"Now really!" She gave me an upper-class frown. "You must know that, officer!"

"Oh, sure. Nothing the captain overlooked?"

"He even took the toothpaste!" She sounded bitter about it, as though she had been out of toothpaste at the time.

It seemed this well was now pumped dry. The time had come for me to do a chore of thinking—of putting together the jigsaw of facts and guesses I had managed to accumulate during the past two hours or so. The place for that was behind my scarred oak desk on the eighth floor of the Clawson Building, with only the telephone and this month's Varga girl for company. . . .

I stood up and retrieved my hat. "We'll keep in touch with you, Mrs. Van Cleve. Don't bother seeing me to the door."

She hadn't intended to. She gave me a blank lidless stare and moved one of the white pomponed mules about an inch and folded her hands in the lap of her bathrobe.

While I was turning the doorknob Gilbert looked up from where he sat slumped on the day bed and gave me a full-lipped sneer. I took my hand off the knob and bent and picked up the blueberry-stained plate and dropped it on the blanket next to one of his legs. I said, "Wear it in your buttonhole, Junior. So the girls will know you."

He didn't move. I went past him and quietly along the hall to the porch. Above the wind I could hear him yelling words at her but all they amounted to was noise.

I waited until I got back downtown before having an early dinner. I ate at the Ontra near Adams Street, not far from the office. They had fresh blueberry pie among the desserts.

But not for me.

CHAPTER 13

At six-thirty I was back in my office, standing at the window, its shade drawn all the way up and Jackson Boulevard spread out below me. The sun was gone behind the uneven line of towering buildings at the Loop's western edge, leaving the sky there a harsh gritty red from layers of dust kicked up by the wind.

The evening rush hour had already tapered to a trickle. Late shoppers and the folks who did the locking up were edging out cautiously into the bludgeoning wind, holding desperately to hats and packages. The newsstands had their backs up, horseshoes and strings with weights tied to the ends holding down the papers. There was no sound beyond the lonely keening wail of the wind among the cornices and setbacks of the stone jungle.

It was an evening for taking in a movie, for sitting in a bar, for shooting hooligan at the corner cigar store. It was an evening for going home and having the radio on without really hearing it while you drank highballs over a book by Roy Huggins or Kenneth Patchen or some other streamlined intellectual.

I left the window open a crack from the bottom and sat down at the desk and leafed through a late edition of the *Daily News*. The cone of light from the desk lamp looked pale and artificial under the fading daylight from the window behind me. From down the corridor came the clatter of mop buckets and the dim echoes of a laugh that had its roots somewhere east of the Vistula.

The phone rang.

A woman's voice—a voice I didn't recognize. "Mr. Pine?"

"That's right."

"Are you alone?"

"There might be a fly or two around," I said. "Who is this?"

"Your good deed for the day—Susan Griswold. This is the third time I've called you this afternoon. I was beginning to think they'd thrown you in a dungeon or something." Her voice had the light, unhurried, very clear way of speaking they seem to teach in finishing schools.

"They couldn't be bothered," I said. "They sat me down and asked me some questions. Not many—not nearly so many as they would if Mary Conrad had amounted to anything."

"That's not a very nice thing to say."

"Tell it to them," I said. "It's the way they look at it."

After a short pause she said, "Was I left out of the conversation? Or did your change of heart fall through?"

"As far as I know," I said, "you're in the clear. If they know about you it didn't come from me."

"How else *could* they know?"

"I haven't any idea how much work is going into their investigation," I said. "The district captain's in charge and he acts too dumb to be anything but smart. If he runs this all the way to the Tropicabana he may come up with the fact that the dead woman was once very thick with your stepmother. From there he could arrive at the fact that you don't like your stepmother and that you had been seen talking to Mary Conrad. From there he could go in any one of several directions, depending on how much help he got."

There was the sound of an unsteady breath against my ear, but when she spoke again her voice was unruffled. "You don't actually think he's that smart, do you?"

I turned a page of the *News* with my free hand and looked at an advertisement showing a boy and a girl leaning on the rail of a boat under a full moon. They were talking about what the right cigarette could do for one of their zones.

"I went straight home," Susan Griswold was saying, sounding suddenly very far away. "*She* wasn't there. At home, I mean."

"Where are you calling from?" I asked.

"A drugstore booth. There's no one around."

"Well, my wire isn't tapped either. You're telling me your stepmother wasn't at home when Mary Conrad was killed?"

"That's right. She left right after lunch and didn't get back until less than an hour ago. You see what that can mean, don't you?"

"It can mean whatever you want it to mean, Miss Griswold. Is that why you called me?"

"Partly. And partly because I got to thinking about what you said this afternoon. You know—about Eve being afraid that Mary Conrad might say too much to me."

"Uh-hunh," I said. She was leading up to something: the tone of her voice telegraphed it.

"Well, you tried so hard to sell me on the idea that I started wondering why, and that led to something else."

"And what would that be, Miss Griswold?"

"To what you were doing in that apartment this afternoon."

"Oh—that."

"You didn't tell me, you know," she said reproachfully. "So I tried to figure it out for myself. I think I did pretty well, too. Would you like to hear what I figured out?"

She made it sound sweet and deadly—like a five-pound box

of chocolate creams loaded with curare. "By all means," I said cordially. "By—all—means!"

"I decided," she said, "that your reason for being there was the same as mine—that you wanted information about Eve Griswold. Only you didn't know then that her name was Eve Griswold!"

"Try it once more," I said flatly. "This time through left tackle."

"Very funny!" she snapped, dropping the mask. "You know what I mean. When I started telling you about Eve it was all you could do to stay awake—until I happened to mention that she once roomed with Mary Conrad. I thought you were going to fall off the couch! You put on a poker face to end all poker faces, and you wanted to know if Eve had roomed with her at the Surf Street apartment or where. And it wasn't two minutes after that that you were trying your damnedest to talk me into turning Eve over to the police for murder! How'm I doing, Mr. Pine?"

"Your badge will go out in tonight's mail, Miss Griswold."

"Oh, there's more," she said sweetly. "I wouldn't want a badge just because of my 'stunning figure and nice honest eyes'—if you don't mind being quoted. No, you ended up by letting me go—after so carefully pointing out earlier what the police could do to you for doing it—but you said you'd expect a favor in return . . . I guess that's about all I can think of right now."

"One minor point," I said. "Since I was out to get your stepmother, wouldn't it have been smart to hang on to you until the cops came—then tell them the story?"

"You were too intelligent to do that," she said admiringly. "You realized Eve is married to thirty million dollars. No policeman is going to fight that much money—not unless there's more to go on than a fancy story handed out by a private detective. If you could have talked me into backing you up, it might have worked out—without me you were licked. . . . Are you still there, Mr. Pine?"

"I'm here," I growled. "Nothing's happened to drive me away. You must have some reason for telling me all this, or are you the gloating type?"

"Don't take it so hard," she said, amused. "I thought we might work on this together—my way."

"Doing what?"

"I want the truth about Eve Shelby Griswold," she said, no longer amused. "And I think you do too, after what happened this afternoon."

I said, "Does the name Ellen Purcell mean anything to you?"

"No-o-o. Should it?"

"How about Laura Fremont, alias Louise Fairchild?"

"No."

"Grace Rehak?"

"I'm sorry but it's still no. Who—?"

"Okay," I said. "We'll work together, if that's what you want. Your first job is to get me a good clear photograph of Eve Griswold. One of these cabinet-sized pictures will do the trick."

"Well, I suppose I . . . " Her voice faded away and there was a lengthy silence from the other end of the wire. "That's funny," she said finally. "Come to think of it, I don't remember seeing any pictures of Eve around. . . . Paul!"

"Yeah?"

"You know something? There *aren't* any pictures of her! I mean it! Father wanted some wedding photographs made but she kept putting it off and they never were taken. Even the papers weren't allowed to take any pictures at the wedding. Doesn't that prove she—?"

"Not necessarily," I cut in. "The camera's no good for

some people. Well, nice having you in the firm, Miss Griswold. Get in touch with me in a day or two and I'll let you know how we're doing."

She sensed the dismissal in my tone. "Wait a minute," she protested. "Isn't there something *I* can be doing?"

"You bet there is," I said. "You can keep out of this. Two women have had the nylon treatment already, and I don't want you ending up wearing three stockings!"

"*Two* women?" she echoed. "But I thought Mary Conrad was the——"

"Not over the phone," I said. "Anyway it's past our closing time. Thanks for calling, Miss Griswold, and good-by."

I dropped the receiver back where it belonged and sat there and stared at my nails. Quite a girl—Susan Griswold. Lovely enough to rest the eyes of any man. A little stiff in the back and high in the nose, but that could come from having three stepmothers in rapid order, none of them what you'd call the motherly type. Inclined to be suspicious of people and their motives, probably for the same reason. And a nice gift for logic, judging from the conversation just finished.

I broke the cellophane on a fresh pack of cigarettes, lighted one and leaned back to put my heels on the blotter. What was supposed to be a simple case of skip-tracing was now as complicated as Blackstone on Torts.

Still, I had made some progress. Laura Fremont had once roomed with Mary Conrad, whose present address was now the morgue. Grace Rehak had also roomed with Mary Conrad within a few days after Laura had moved out. According to a statement made by Miss Conrad shortly before her death, either Grace Rehak or Laura Fremont had adopted the name Eve Shelby, taken a job at a night club and there met and later married thirty million dollars by the name of Lawrence Griswold.

Both Laura and Gracie had excellent reasons for not wanting their true identity brought out. Laura presumably was wanted for the murder of one Ellen Purcell, a former roommate. Grace was the graduate of a Lincoln, Nebraska, cathouse—not the best reference for the wife of a socially prominent millionaire. The best method of hiding secrets like those is to stop the breathing of anyone in a position to blow the lid off.

The fact that Ellen Purcell and Mary Conrad had died in the same manner would tend to show Laura Fremont as the killer—provided, of course, that Laura had actually knocked off Ellen Purcell. All else being taken into consideration, it seemed Laura, rather than Gracie Rehak, was now the wife of Lawrence Griswold. Laura Fremont had destroyed all pictures of herself before leaving Lincoln; Eve Griswold was also camera shy.

I stood up, creaking a little in the joints, and closed the window. The first shadows of night were beginning to crowd in on the street below and the lights and neon signs were springing up. Under the lash of the wind the sidewalks were almost completely deserted now.

I leaned a shoulder against the frame and kept my thoughts churning. There were other pieces to the pattern, minor perhaps, but still necessary to fit in before the true design could stand out clear and bold. For one, Bertha Lund's interest in my affairs—an interest strong enough for her to send some gowed-up muscle to search my hotel room and, in passing, to bash in the skull of a nice open-faced youngster who had happened to get in the way.

Still another piece—a soiled piece and probably not really important—was the Lesbianism angle that had cropped up during the police investigation of Mary Conrad's murder. Judging from some of the details Mrs. Fremont let out about her daughter, added to the story given by Mrs. Van Cleve, it would seem Laura Fremont did all her swinging at female curves. It didn't help the theory that she was now the wife of Lawrence Griswold, although such things have been known to happen.

I went back to the desk and spat in the wastebasket and sat down again. Two more pieces to the puzzle were Susan Griswold and a well-dressed, clean-necked number who called himself Smith.

Which reminded me. I rummaged through my pockets and came up with what I was after—a matchbook folder with the license number of an automobile scrawled in ink on the inside of the cover.

Mr. Smith need no longer remain the puzzle he was at present. A phone call to a cubbyhole in the Criminal Courts Building out on Twenty-sixth and California would get me the number of whoever owned that big black Cadillac. I thought I already knew who owned it but it would be nice to be sure.

The phone rang sharply while I was reaching for it. I yanked my hand back without intending to and scowled, listening to it ring a second time before I answered.

"Would this be a man named Pine?" a woman's voice drawled. It was a stagy voice, low-pitched, even a little sultry.

"This," I said, "would."

"I don't suppose I have to tell you who this is," the voice went on. "Or do you make a habit of pestering more than one person at a time?"

My fingers tightened slowly against the receiver's chill surface. "Nice of you to call, Miss Rehak. Has my breath been getting a little too hot for you?"

"It's not its heat I object to," she said nastily. "What's all the shooting, mister?"

"No shootings. This time it's stockings. Much quieter."

Out of a small pool of silence she said, "If that means something, I don't know what. Exactly what do you want of me?"

"A few words is all. In person."

"A few words about what?"

"Hunh-uh, Miss Rehak. Not over the wire."

"Listen," she said tightly, "do you think I'm a fool? This sounds like an invitation to be blackmailed. I'm not having any!"

"Are you ripe for blackmail?" I asked.

"Oh, Jesus! Either say what's on your mind or I'm hanging up!"

"I've said what's on my mind. It still goes."

Her words took on an almost deadly calm. "As far as I'm concerned Grace Rehak is dead and buried. I can't risk having anyone see me as Grace Rehak and you know why. I'd be at the mercy of every two-bit grifter that came along afterward."

"Horsefeathers!" I said. "I don't give two hoots in a bathtub if you're the mayor's wife. If I'm going to talk to you at all it'll be face to face. Wear a veil if you want to. Or a section of stovepipe. Or hang up the phone like you've been telling me. I don't mind spending another day or two on the job."

"I've got to know what's going on," she said softly, more to herself than to me. Abruptly her voice was no longer soft. "All right. I'll meet you. But it'll have to be my way."

"I'm listening," I said.

A brief silence while she thought it out. "Where do you live, Pine?"

"The Dinsmore Arms. On Wayne Avenue, a block north of Pratt Boulevard."

"Well. . . . Look, it'll have to be late. I can't get away much before twelve, one o'clock."

"I can always sleep late the next day," I said.

"I'll be in my car," she said. "Parked along one of the side streets near your hotel. You tell me where."

"Farwell Avenue," I said. "Between Wayne and Lakewood, on the south side of the street. Leave your parking lights on. Will you be driving the black Cadillac sedan?"

I heard her breath catch. After a long moment she said, "Maybe I'm being careful for nothing. Or did Stu tell you the make of car I drive? It's not like him to talk so much."

"Stu," I said, "is a clam. But he's a clumsy clam. You plan on bringing him along tonight?"

"No point to that now," she said bitterly. "He's done all he can to help. I thought money was important to you private snoops."

I said, "One o'clock then, Miss Rehak. I'll be on time."

"Wait a minute," she said, her voice sharp now and a little loud. "I warn you I'm going to be carrying a gun. Don't try anything funny!"

"Like what, Miss Rehak?" I said politely.

"Like flashing a light in my face. Or trying to force me to answer questions."

"There will be some questions," I said. "But the answers won't expose your secret past to a cruel and merciless world. Incidentally, Chris sends his regards."

"Who's Chris?" she said suspiciously.

"What're you trying to pull?" I said, just as suspiciously. "I'm talking about your father. Don't tell me he's dead and buried too?"

Her laugh was a short hard burst of sound. "My God, Pine, I'm surprised at you! When it comes to being clever you're really a card. My old man's name is Stanislaus Rehak—cut down to Stanley a long time ago—and he's hated my guts ever since I was fourteen and dating the track captain at high school. When I blew town he was still living in the same stinking dump I grew up in. 322 South Twentieth, across the street from the Lincolnwood Dairy. You want the night foreman's name over there?"

"I'll bet you wouldn't know the day foreman," I muttered.

"I heard that!" she snapped. "Okay, *Mister* Pine, I'll keep our date, at the time and the place you said. After that keep the hell away from me if you want to stay healthy!"

She hung up hard enough to leave me a sore ear. I pushed away the phone and lighted a cigarette and continued to sit, poking the burned matchstick at the folder with the license number written under the flap. I listened to the silence around me and beyond that the whine of the restless wind.

If Grace Rehak was now the wife of thirty million bucks, her language was still from Bertha Lund's parlor house. Or maybe she kept it under the shelf for use on private detectives. Or maybe she wasn't Mrs. Lawrence Griswold at all.

I went back to the phone again and called the number I had started to call earlier.

"H'lo."

"Harvey?" I asked.

"Yeah."

"This is Paul Pine, Harvey. How's it going?"

"Okay."

"I need some help on a small matter," I said. "Can do?"

"Okay."

"Got a license number of a Cadillac. Want the name and address of the party it's registered to."

"Okay."

"Number 376-941. Illinois '48. . . . Got it?"

"Okay."

"Want to call me back, Harvey?"

"Okay."

I gave him my number and hung up. During my years as

an investigator on the staff of the State's Attorney, the rumor was strong that Harvey had once said five words in one sentence. Nobody actually believed it.

In fifteen minutes the phone rang. Harvey at the other end. "Pine?"

"Uh-huh."

"Steven O'Flynn."

"Steven O'Flynn?" I repeated blankly.

"Yeah."

I shrugged. "Okay. Steven O'Flynn. What address?"

"1803 East Fifty-third Street."

I wrote it out under Mary Conrad's name on the calendar pad. "Nice going, Harvey," I said. "How're things around the department?"

"Okay."

"One of these days I'll stop by and say hello."

"Okay."

I cradled the phone, grinning, tore off the calendar sheet and reached for the phone book. It listed no Steven O'Flynn, on Fifty-third or off it. But Fifty-third Street had cropped up before in this case and after a moment I remembered the circumstances. I flipped the pages rapidly to the T's—and two pieces of the puzzle now fitted together.

1803 East Fifty-third Street was listed as the address of the Tropicabana—the night club first mentioned by Susan Griswold earlier in the day. Since then the name had kept cropping up—so many times that something would have to be done about it.

The time was seven-twenty. Tonight was to be my night with Gracie, and Gracie might have all the answers. But it wouldn't hurt to know some of the facts beforehand—facts I could use in prying her loose from some of those answers.

I climbed into my hat and went on out the door.

CHAPTER 14

THE Tropicabana turned out to be a narrow high-shouldered firetrap of two floors with gray stucco walls, a blinker sign on the roof and the air of impermanence common to all night clubs. I drove slowly past the entrance, left the Plymouth in a corner parking lot and allowed the gale to blow me along the walk and up to the front door.

The foyer was large, with a tropical *décor* that would fool nobody south of the Arctic Circle. There were a lot of people in party clothes and the air smelled of face powder and the fragrance of good perfume and the odor of rich cigars.

Business was good enough for them to have the velvet rope up and a line waiting. A silver-haired captain of waiters stood at attention behind the rope, a packet of menus the size of billboards under one arm, the other hand ready in case somebody wanted to slip something green in it. Beyond him was a broad swath of white-clothed tables, and beyond that a dance floor and a platform holding a small orchestra in bright blouses and skintight trousers flaring at the knee.

At the straight ledge of the checkroom a curved brunette in a Hollywood sarong gave me a square of blue pasteboard in exchange for my hat. I looked at her empty smile and said, "Where do I find Steven O'Flynn?"

She said, "The boss? You'll have to ask Mr. Carter, sir." She pointed a flame-colored fingernail at a pair of velvet draperies on the opposite wall. I crossed over to them and pushed one aside and went into a shallow recess where a man sat behind a kneehole desk that held a lamp, a telephone and nothing else.

The man was slender and quiet-faced, a little on the elderly side, and they were letting him wear a dinner suit instead of a sarong. He gave me a gravely impersonal smile, hid his distress at my lack of dinner clothes and said, "May I help you, sir?" like a floorman in Ladies' Ready-to-Wear.

"The name's Pine," I told him. "To see Mr. O'Flynn."

A freshly manicured set of nails rose gracefully and settled on the telephone. But that was as far as it went. "Is Mr. O'Flynn expecting you, Mr. Pine?"

"Hunh-uh."

"What did you wish to see Mr. O'Flynn about?"

"A personal matter."

The eyes slid slowly from my face to my coat, found no suspicious bulges under either arm, then crawled slowly back to my bright and cheerful countenance. "Mr. O'Flynn," he said gently, "will want to know something of the nature of your call. I'm afraid that will be necessary, sir."

"And quite right," I said. "Tell him it's about a black Cadillac sedan—his."

There might have been a wrinkle in the smooth skin of his forehead by now, but it was gone before I could be sure. He lifted the receiver without haste, pressed one of several buttons set in the standard, waited ten seconds, then said, "Carter, Mr. O'Flynn. In the lobby. A Mr. Pine wishes to see you about one of your cars. The Cadillac sedan. No, sir. Shall I ask—? Yes, sir."

The receiver went back as silently as a snowflake falling on a wool blanket. Without looking at me the man put a finger under the edge of the desk. A faint whirring sound followed and a section of the paneled wall behind him slid aside, letting me see the door of a small self-service elevator.

I hadn't expected anything like that. I looked from the elevator to the man behind the desk. In his quiet way he was enjoying my expression.

"Second floor," he murmured. "Third door on the left."

"That's quite a gadget you got there," I said. "Just the thing for these long winter evenings."

He smiled his impersonal smile and said nothing. I went past him into the elevator and leaned a thumb against the only button in sight. The panel slid into place, sealing me off in a silent cell, and the cage went up as smoothly as lifting your hand.

Up there was a narrow corridor carpeted in soft gray between walls of soft yellow. Even the doorknobs along it looked soft. I turned left and counted off three of them and knocked. The lock clicked and I pushed open the door and walked in.

Not the night-club office you see in high-budget pictures. No Cezanne originals on leather walls, no long-fringed Orientals, no baroque magnificence. Just three fluted-glass windows along one wall, battleship linoleum underfoot, a few straight chairs, an adding machine on a stand, a battered swivel chair between a piano-legged oak table and an early American roll-top desk against the far wall. In the swivel chair, watching me come toward him, was a medium-bald man in shirt sleeves.

He gave me a long dispassionate stare out of bland blue eyes, took a bulldog briar pipe out of his lipless mouth and pointed its stem at a chair near the oak table.

"Rest yourself," he said in a clear baritone voice. "I'm afraid I don't have the pleasure of your acquaintance. I'm O'Flynn, Steven O'Flynn. With a V," he added, as if he expected to find an account of our meeting written up in tomorrow's paper.

I was in the chair by this time, looking at him across the table. He was a barrel-chested, slope-shouldered Irishman who could have been five years on either side of fifty. His round, pink-skinned face was as hard as a jail-house wall, with small blunt features and a fringe of sandy hair bordering a naked pate. The flesh-colored button of a hearing aid was screwed into his right ear, its wire running under the soft collar of his white shirt. I hoped I wouldn't have to yell at him.

He said, "What's this crack about my Caddy, Pine?"

I said, "I had a visitor this afternoon. A man named Smith. After he left, a car picked him up. It was your car, Mr. O'Flynn."

"What about it?"

"I'm anxious to get in touch with Mr. Smith," I said. "He overlooked leaving his address with me at the time and picking him out of the phone book would be kind of difficult. Then I thought of his using your car, so I figured you'd be the one to help me."

Light moved along his pale eyes as his gaze shifted to the pipe in his hand. "I don't know anybody named Smith. You've made a mistake somewhere along the line."

"Everybody," I said, "knows somebody named Smith. There's too many of them not to. But I don't think this guy's name is Smith at all."

His jaw hardened. "Then what the hell do you expect me to do? Tell you about a man whose name you don't know?"

"It was your car," I said. "I assume you'd know who you lent it to."

He looked at me stonily for a long moment. Behind his lack of expression thoughts were being born. "You said it different before," he pointed out. "A minute ago you mentioned that a car, my car, had picked Smith up. That sounds like somebody else was behind the wheel."

"A woman was driving."

"A woman," he said tonelessly. "You didn't say that before."

I got out my cigarettes and matches. O'Flynn dug a Woolworth ash tray from a welter of adding-machine tape and cancelled dinner checks and pushed it over where I could reach. He picked up a mechanical pencil from the same dime store and made a meaningless mark on a scratch pad and put it down again and leaned his folded arms on the table, waiting for me to say more. In the silence the rustle of marimbas came faintly into the room from the first floor.

"Okay," I said. "Let's talk about the woman instead. Did she borrow your car this afternoon?"

"Borrowed is hardly the word," he said evenly. "It so happens that Caddy belongs to my wife."

"Sorry I bothered you," I said, preparing to stand up. "Mrs. O'Flynn will be the one for me to see then. Does she happen to be here tonight?"

"Sit still, Pine." His voice was cold and his eyes far colder. He unfolded his arms and knocked the dead ashes from his pipe into the ash tray. He turned the swivel chair and reached a tin of tobacco from the roll-top and began filling the bowl with slow care. Light from behind the frosted glass of the ceiling fixture glinted on the reddish fuzz covering the backs of his hands.

"What's behind all this yapping?" he said. "You a cop?"

"The private kind," I said. "No authority, nothing to back me up. No reason why I can't be thrown out. If that's what you want."

He struck a match and held it to the pipe, eying me over

the flame as it sank and rose under his inhalations. He blew out the match with a gust of smoke and continued to hold it between two fingers.

"Tell me some more about this man Smith," he said casually. "What's your interest in him?"

"I'm looking for a certain woman. He knows where she is."

"What's her name?"

"Grace Rehak."

His expression said the name meant nothing to him. "What does she look like?"

"I never saw her, Mr. O'Flynn. I've heard her described, but it might be the wrong description."

"Let's hear it anyway."

"Small, black-haired, brown eyes. Figure like a boy's is the way I got it."

He shook his head slightly. "That could fit any one of a million. What do you want her for?"

"I have to hold back something," I said. "That's the part I'm holding back."

His wrist jerked sharply, throwing the match on the floor, and he leaned forward and stared at me through narrowed lids. "You said Smith called on you today. Wouldn't he tell you where to find her?"

"No."

"Why wouldn't he?"

"It seems she's changed her name," I said, "and doesn't want her present identity to be hooked up with the old one."

"When did this switch take place?"

"Can't say exactly. Not more than two years back and maybe much more recently."

His lipless mouth was a white-edged straight line now. "Why did she have to take on a new name? And who hired you to find her?"

"We're back to that part I can't talk about, Mr. O'Flynn."

He showed me his teeth in what wasn't a smile. "On your feet, wise guy," he said clearly. "Take the air. Crawl on out. And stay away from my wife if you like living."

"What's the matter?" I said, staying where I was. "Has she got black hair and brown eyes?"

His face turned so red it bleached out his hair. He came out of his chair and around the desk at me, his hands balled into fists. On the outside I didn't move a muscle and my grin was as steady as I could make it.

"Throwing me out won't change things," I said. "Even if I let you. If it turns out your wife is Grace Rehak, as you seem to think she might be, the sooner we find out the better."

He stood over me, breathing hard enough for me to hear it. Muscles crawled on the underside of his jaw. "Keep on talking," he said in a strangled voice. "Get it out while you've still got a tongue to wag."

"Two words will do it," I said. "Mary Conrad."

He kept on scowling but it was suddenly a puzzled scowl. "Mary Conrad?" he repeated. "Who? . . . Wait a minute. You mean that black-haired little hoofer in the show downstairs?"

"Uh-hunh."

"What about her? How does she figure in this?"

"She was murdered about three o'clock this afternoon."

He backed away from me sharply, his hip striking hard against the table. He stood there for a long moment, not saying anything, his mouth open slightly, a muscle twitching lightly in one cheek. Then he turned and moved carefully around behind the table and sat down and picked up his pipe.

When I saw his eyes again it was as though a curtain had been drawn across them. "I'm sorry to hear that, Pine. Mary had been with us for quite a while. The police know about it?"

"Yeah."

"How did it happen?"

"A woman's stocking was twisted around her neck in her apartment. A woman did the job. At least that's the police theory. They found a hunk of lace torn from a woman's underthings in one of her hands."

"How come you know about it? From the papers?"

"If it's in the papers I didn't see it. No. I was there."

"Ahead of the cops?"

I nodded. "I'm the lucky guy who found her."

He didn't say anything. I took out a cigarette and lighted it with an airy gesture and a match. I said, "You haven't asked me why she was murdered, Mr. O'Flynn, but I'll tell you my theory if you like."

"And if I don't like," he said sourly, "I'll hear it anyway. Go ahead."

I blew out some smoke and watched it drift toward the ceiling. "In one way or another word has got around that I'm looking for the former Grace Rehak. There are some people who know her under two names—or there were. One was Mary Conrad. I told you what happened to her. Maybe another was a girl named Ellen Purcell. A third is still another dame: Laura Fremont, alias Louise Fairchild. Number four, for a change, is a man—a man who calls himself Smith. Any of those names strike a familiar chord? Other than Mary Conrad, that is?"

"Not that I know of," he said quickly. Too quickly.

"Sure you do," I said. "Ellen Purcell. She worked here. But the cops never came around on that one, did they? That was because she wasn't a girl to do a lot of gabbing about herself. But I think she knew Gracie Rehak—and she died. Mary Conrad worked for you and knew Gracie Rehak—and *she* died. The coincidences, as you can see, are piling up."

In the silence the wind went past the fluted-glass windows with a sound like the Hoboken Express. The man across the table sat with his head cocked slightly to one side as though listening to the tiny voices of leprechauns.

He said, almost with an effort: "Let's have the rest of it, shamus."

"You already know the rest of it. Today the mysterious Mr. Smith drops in to buy the reason for my interest in Grace Rehak. Not that you care, but what he got you could put in a microbe's left ventricle. So he stalks out of my office and climbs in a black Cadillac sedan piloted by a black-haired woman—a woman who answers Grace Rehak's description. That, Mr. O'Flynn, is one coincidence too many."

I stopped and took a long deep drag from my cigarette and watched him hate me. He said savagely, "Well, what are you waiting for—applause?"

I said, "I'd like a few words with your wife."

His lip curled in a tight, tough-Irish sneer. "What for? You going to sit there and tell me she's this Rehak babe, just because she happens to have the same color hair and knows a friend of Rehak's? You haven't any idea how much I know about my wife."

"If you knew she couldn't be Grace Rehak," I said, "I'd have been out of here on my ear ten minutes ago. But there's always the chance that she's not. Why don't we find out, one way or the other, before the cops come around and find out for us?"

His eyes took on a sleepy look, as eyes do in some circles when it's time to get tough. "So you're going to yell copper, hunh? That's supposed to scare me. Me—with the games I run down the hall. Look, fellow, I got more cops on my payroll than you can count. You think for one goddam minute they're going to give Steve O'Flynn a bad time just to please some three-for-a-quarter private dick?"

"The boys in your district," I said, "keep what you pay them. None of it gets into Central Homicide and you know it. When those babies get a lead on a killing they milk it dry —and you won't mean any more to them than any other grifter."

I stood up and dropped my cigarette into the ash tray. "Thanks for letting me waste your time, Mr. O'Flynn," I said and turned and started for the door.

I made about half the distance before his voice reached me. "You forgot to put out that cigarette, Pine."

He was still chilly, still tough. But I didn't believe it any more. I turned around and walked slowly back and used a matchstick to extinguish the glowing coal. Then I sat down in the chair again and crossed my legs and kept my face blank.

He was lighting his pipe, taking his time about it. Nobody was going to hurry him. I waited. I could afford to wait, now.

He dropped the match on the floor and spoke around the bit of his pipe, his voice almost gentle. "You're going to have that talk with my wife. I don't know what she'll tell you and I care even less. But if she does give you anything the cops can use and they get it afterward, you'll come down with a case of lead ulcers, my friend."

"And I'm so young," I said sadly.

He turned his back on me and grabbed the phone and pushed a button. "Frank? See if Bonnie's in the bar. Yeah? Well, pry the glass out of her fist and get her up here. Right now."

He slammed down the receiver and swung around. Before he could say anything I said, "I'll want to talk to her alone, Mr. O'Flynn."

He couldn't believe his ears. "You must be out of your mind!" he snarled. "You think for a minute I'm going to hand my wife over to you so you can shove her into a murder rap? Bonnie's not what I thought a wife should be, but she's still my wife and I'm not going to toss her to the wolves. You'll talk to her with me five feet away or by God you won't talk to her at all!"

I said, "You're getting me mixed up with the homicide boys. All I want is information, not to solve any murders. Head her off and advise her not to confess to any and she'll be all right. Only I want the information I want and while you're at it tell her so."

He went back over it, thinking. "Then all this talk about her being Grace Rehak was for what?"

"You're getting confused," I said. "If she's Grace Rehak that still doesn't prove she killed anybody. It just proves she might have a reason for it—and that's different. Any lawyer will tell you as much."

It took almost a minute for him to make up his mind. Then he stood up heavily and came around the desk and put his face close to mine. "Double-cross me on this and I'll have you at the bottom of the lake, Pine," he almost whispered.

"You said almost the same thing a few minutes ago," I reminded him. "Stop trying to scare me. You succeeded a long time ago."

He turned on his heel and went over to the door and out.

CHAPTER 15

SHE came in and closed the door harder than necessary and leaned against it, eying me with a mixture of interest and insolence. A cigarette smoldered at the corner of her too-red mouth and she was squinting slightly against the smoke. She had been at the bottle a couple of snorts too long but she carried it with the ease of long practice. Under a flame-red, very tight evening dress her hips showed with smooth emphasis and she carried her breasts high and insistent, like medals won in combat.

I said, "Nice of you to come up, Mrs. O'Flynn. I expect your husband told you why."

"He didn't say." Her voice had a brassy ring. "Just that a private cop named Pine had some questions."

"That mean anything to you?"

She curled a lip at me. She took the cigarette out of her face so the lip could curl even better. "Not a thing. Steve said to see you and I'm seeing you. What'll it be?"

"Why don't we sit down, Mrs. O'Flynn?"

She came over to the table and leaned a rounded hip against it. "I left a friend in the bar. Let's get it over with."

"Not Stu again?" I said. "What will your husband say?"

I got the full treatment from a pair of brown eyes as round and as blank as a child's. But that didn't mean they were the eyes of a child. "Don't start off with riddles, handsome. You got something to say, say it."

It appeared all of O'Flynn's taste was in his mouth. She was an inch or two over five feet but it took spike heels to put her there. She was too thin in the legs, you could knit a sweater with her arms and her waist looked like somebody's thumb. Her dark hair had a beauty-shop curl and she wore it piled on top where it would look the worst. You see dozens like her around hotel lounges and cocktail bars any afternoon of any week—pretty in a standard way, shrill in the voice, feverish of eye and hard around the mouth.

I said, "How long have you been around the Tropicabana?"

"Year—year 'n a half. Why?"

"How long you been married to O'Flynn?"

"Didn't he tell you?"

"I didn't ask him. How long, Mrs. O'Flynn?"

"Four months ago."

"What was your name before that?"

She narrowed her eyes. "What're you getting at?"

"All in good time, lady. The name was——"

"Bonnie Field."

I remembered a name plate above an apartment bell. M. Conrad. B. Field. I moved my tongue along my suddenly dry lips and stared hard at her. Her mouth twisted slightly under my stare, whether with annoyance or fear I couldn't tell.

I said, "Remember Ellen Purcell, Bonnie?"

"What about her?" The words came quickly, as if she had expected the question.

"How well did you know her?"

"She worked here. So do sixteen other women, counting the powder-room maid."

"The way I hear it, you two were plenty thick."

"I can't help what you hear."

"What do I have to do, knock it out of you?"

She leaned toward me and said swiftly, "Okay. I knew Ellen; sure I knew her. And I know what happened to her. But that's all I know and you're not mixing me up in no murder!"

I shook my head. "It's the other way around. I'm trying to keep you out of it. But maybe I'm not going to be able to."

She said thinly, "I'd love to know how you're not going to keep me out of it. I really would."

"The police," I said, "didn't make a first down on that job. It wasn't an important killing to begin with and there was nothing for them to get hold of, no starting point. Why? Because Ellen Purcell and her roommate were Lesbians and, as such, kept strictly to themselves, made no friends in the neighborhood and were careful not to be talked about. Even the landlady didn't catch on—and she's a dame that would try."

I waited for Bonnie O'Flynn to comment. But she had retreated into a shell, and only the sudden flare of color in her cheeks and the stiffness of her fingers on her cigarette hinted at what she was thinking.

"I've been hired to find a girl," I said. "She's one of four who came together a couple of years ago and who have more or less stuck together since then. That is they stuck together up until January of this year. That was when Ellen Purcell moved into the cemetery."

The hand holding the cigarette came up slowly and put it betwen the overripe lips in the thin face. Smoke ballooned out and drifted slowly down the room. Outside, the wind strummed the building eaves and rattled the window frames.

"That left three," I said. "Mary Conrad, Grace Rehak, Laura Fremont. Only now, as of today, there are only two. In case your husband didn't tell you, Mary Conrad died about three this afternoon."

Except for the sharp flaring of her thin nostrils she might have been cut from a block of granite. After nearly thirty seconds of that, the muscles in her throat moved as she swallowed almost convulsively. "Why tell me all this?" she croaked.

"Why?" I said. "I'll tell you why. Because Grace Rehak has been told I'm looking for her. Mary Conrad was pushed for fear she'd tell me where I could find Grace Rehak. A smooth lad named Smith came to see me about Grace Rehak. He rode away in a car driven by a woman who answered the description of Grace Rehak. The car was a black Cadillac sedan owned by Steven O'Flynn. Where does that put *you*, Mrs. O'Flynn?"

"So you think I'm Grace Rehak." Her voice was flat, emotionless.

"Are you?"

"No."

"You may have to prove it. The name B. Field is on the bell at Mary Conrad's apartment."

"I never lived there. I used it as a mailing address."

"The cops know the Conrad woman worked here. They'll want to know who B. Field is. Don't think they won't find out—if they try."

"Let them find out. I've got nothing to hide. I can prove I'm not Grace Rehak. You said she's the one who killed Mary."

"Not exactly. I said she didn't want to be found. But let's say you're not Grace Rehak. The fact remains that you know her and you'll never be able to make me believe you don't. You knew Mary Conrad and Ellen Purcell and you know the man called Smith—and he knows Grace Rehak, who knows Laura Fremont."

She took a deep drag at her cigarette, letting the smoke trickle out slowly. "I told you I'm not Grace Rehak and I'll prove it when the time comes to prove it. Now what do you want?"

"Two girls left," I said, looking into her eyes. "Grace Rehak and Laura Fremont. One of them is the one I was hired to find. But I'll take them both, Mrs. O'Flynn. Where do I find them?"

Her eyes were hard and shiny now, like sandstone in a river bed. "You'd like to know, wouldn't you? You think all you have to do to get me to rat on my friends is come around and ask. Only I might get a little stubborn, so you figure to soften me up first by throwing in some fast talk about murder and the cops!"

She made a quarter-turn and ground out her cigarette with savage jabbing motions of her hand. Then she turned back and gave me the rest of the speech.

"Well, this time you miss out, bright boy. I haven't seen or heard from Grace Rehak in months. The same goes for Laura Fremont. And even if I had, even if I could tell you and your tongue was hanging out waiting, you'd never get it from me! Not even the right time if you were starving!"

By the time she finished her voice was bouncing off the walls and her hands were fists and her breath quick and shallow. I stood there watching her in a detached, fifth-row-center way, not moving, not saying anything, just watching. After a while it began to get under her skin. I should have been yelling back at her or chewing the rug or trying to crawl under the table.

The hands unballed slowly and she took a cigarette from a box on the table. I had a match burning before she knew she needed one. We looked into each other's eyes across the flame. Mine would never be as hard as hers.

She straightened and took the cigarette from her mouth, holding it cupped in her hand, the way few women hold a cigarette. Her eyes were cold where they had been blazing only a moment before. "Will that be all, Mr. Pine. I really must be getting back."

"I was just thinking," I said. "Seeing a picture, sort of. A room down at Eleventh and State where the boys in blue hang their hats. The homicide boys sitting around in a circle. A few run-of-the-mill plain-clothes men and a sergeant or two, with the lieutenant looking in now and then. You're in a chair in the center of that circle, Mrs. O'Flynn. It's a hard chair, an uncomfortable chair, and you've been sitting in it for a long time. There's a light in the room but it's not too bright and it's not shining in your eyes. They don't go in for that much any more. But they've asked you what I've just finished asking, and you've given them the same answer."

"It would have to be the same answer," she said sullenly. "There's no other answer I could give, cops or no cops. Let's not go over that again."

"Not for anything," I said. "Not the way you carry on. You wouldn't know, but I worked out of the State's Attorney office awhile back. I remember once they brought in a nance on suspicion of murder. There's nothing a big muscle-bound hairy-chested cop hates more than a queen. There are books to tell you why, if you don't know why. Well, that suspect copped a plea, mumbling his few words through puffed lips. Two days later he was a lifer at Joliet. The judge would have given a better hearing on a parking violation.

"My point is, that nance never killed anybody, Mrs. O'Flynn. I'd bet on it."

She was frowning. A thoughtful frown that lay like a shadow across her thin face. "I can't see what . . ." She let the words hang there, not finishing, not knowing how to finish.

"You will if you open your eyes," I said. "Police officers

have the habit of thinking that people who hang out with queers are also queer. Let them find out Ellen Purcell and Laura Fremont were Lesbians, just as your other friend Mary Conrad was, and your name on her apartment bell, and the collective mind of those cops is going to be made up mighty quick. They could decide *you* put that stocking around Ellen Purcell's neck, because of what they could think you are. An unshakable alibi could save you, but after eight or nine months almost any alibi would be as shaky as the bed in a bridal suite. The motive would be jealousy, and by the time the boys got done with their carpenter work they'd have a frame to fit you."

Her red-coated lips came slowly unstuck, like a bandage peeling away from an open wound. "And you'd do it too," she said contemptuously. "You'd throw me right in their laps simply because you think I'm holding out on you. How good do you sleep nights, mister ex-cop?"

This was fun. Hit her again, Pine; she's only five feet of dumb broad and one more will do it. I was enjoying this. Every stinking minute of it.

I walked two yards away from her and back again. The wind still shouted in the streets and between gusts I could hear faraway dance music and the thin high note of a woman's laugh strained through walls.

"You're forgetting something," she said suddenly. "You're forgetting I'm married and queer women don't marry men. The police know that, even if you don't. That's why all this fast talk of yours about them suspecting me is just a cheap trick to make me stool on a friend."

"I'm forgetting nothing," I said. "Queers marry for money or for safety or for any one of fifty reasons. Being married to O'Flynn won't get you out of this that easy. Take my word for it."

The contempt was still strong in her voice. "You don't care how you get results, do you? Blackmail, threats—the works. Just so you can earn your stinking whatever-it-amounts-to a day."

"I do my job," I said, my voice dull in my ears. "Make up your mind, Mrs. O'Flynn. Do I get what I want from you the easy way or do I have to use the cops as a club? You've done a lot of slick yammering about ratting on friends. I say at least one of your friends is a killer and needs to be ratted on. Which is it going to be, you or her?"

She opened her hand and deliberately let her cigarette drop to the floor. It hit the linoleum and rolled toward me. The lipstick at one end was like blood on a sheet.

"You win, copper," she said calmly. "I'll see that you get what you're asking for. But it won't be now because I don't know the answer. But I'll get it and when I do you'll hear from me. You'll have it by tomorrow. Early tomorrow."

Our eyes locked for a long moment before she looked down at her hands. "How will I get in touch with you?" she said, making it sound unimportant.

I told her. She heard me through, then gave a short cool nod and walked around me and on out the door, not slamming it this time.

I stayed where I was, leaning against the chair, watching smoke from my cigarette curl upward in a twisting spiral. "You won't last much longer," I said aloud. The words were gall to my tongue.

The cigarette didn't say anything. Nobody had spoken to it.

CHAPTER 16

THE game room was something to see. O'Flynn might skimp on office furnishings but when it came to slicking up for the trade the best was something you hauled in by the truckload.

Not that it was big enough for fleet maneuvers. But still enough room for three roulette layouts down the center under a mammoth crystal chandelier. Along the side walls and in the corners were such things as dice tables and blackjack stations. Powdered shoulders and white ties were thick around the roulette tables, although the one in the center was getting the heavy play. The motionless air carried the crisp rattle of chips, the dry even murmur of croupiers, the shrill voices of women. Put almost any woman in an evening gown and stick a glass in her hand and her voice automatically goes up three octaves. Change the glass for a stack of chips and the walls ring.

I sat on a chrome-and-red-plastic bar stool and sipped at a double cognac and admired the room, if not the people in it. The bar itself filled a long shallow alcove in one of the lemon-colored walls, and here and there along the others, under hooded display lamps, were somber oil paintings which no one bothered to look at. Carpeting the color of a Hanoverian nosebleed ran to the baseboard, deep enough to ambush tigers in.

I finished my drink, wiped my hands with the handkerchief

from my breast pocket and lighted a cigarette. My thoughts were beginning to catch up with me, adding to the gloom brought on by my talk with Bonnie O'Flynn. I thought of Laura Fremont and Grace Rehak, reluctantly, without pleasure and without hope. One of them had probably killed two women. Almost certainly, in fact. I looked at my wrist watch and didn't see what time it was. I remembered the girl on the bed, with her eyes sticking out and four broad shallow scratches across the pale skin of the belly. I remembered Captain Blauvelt's remarks about the twilight zone of sex Mary Conrad and her friends were a part of.

Be a private detective. Easy enjoyable work. See the world through a garbage can. Nuts!

"Another, sir?" asked the barman, holding my empty glass in one clean white hand. He seemed a little worried by my expression. You never know about these solitary drinkers.

"Yeah," I growled. "I got a bad taste in my ears."

It made no sense to him but it did to me. He filled the glass from the same bottle of Delamain and went away for my change. The smoke from my cigarette hung in the tired air like fog in a valley.

I leaned my back against the bar and watched the clump of fancy people around the center roulette table. I had nothing better to do. Two women—young and dressed to gamble—seemed the center of attraction there. A redhead and a blonde. Not much of them was visible, just bare shoulders and wearing their hair the way hair was being worn that season. They would be beautiful, probably, with the enameled, assembly-line kind of beauty that went with hormone creams and Dior gowns.

I decided I was getting too much out of too little.

There was a man with them—a man of medium height, with capable-looking shoulders under the coat of a midnight blue tuxedo cut by an archangel with three centuries to do the job. He seemed to be splitting his time between placing bets and conferring with the redhead. Whenever he spoke to her it brought on a shifting of bodies and a craning of necks as the spectators eavesdropped. His black hair was cropped fairly close and at the moment could have used a comb. Patches of silver at the temples indicated he was old enough to go out with girls.

A man and a woman came out of the crowd at the tables and stood at the bar next to me. He ordered drinks in a loud, almost feverish voice. "I've heard of systems," he said to the woman. "But not like that one I didn't. He doubles at the right time and he drags down at the right time and it all comes out of that book. You're seeing roulette, baby!"

"Lot it means," the woman said, her voice like a damp finger across glass. "Not the way that blonde keeps shoving it back. You know who they are, Herb. Lawrence Griswold and that fourth wife of his. She's certainly common enough."

"My God! You dames!"

They finished their drinks in a hurry and scurried back to the center table. And that was when I got my second look of the day at Mr. Smith.

He was pushing through the crowd, a highball in each hand, his handsome dark head gleaming under the light. I couldn't mistake him. He was wearing dinner clothes that made him look as slender as a steel blade. He put one of the glasses in front of the blonde and said something to her.

I drank the rest of my drink and went over there, my pulses starting to stir. It took some polite shoving before I could get where I wanted to be. Mr. Smith could see me now by turning his head a few inches to the right. That would be fine. I would enjoy having him see me.

The redhead wasn't betting. She was a tall unfrail number

in her twenties, wearing her hair drawn back in a smooth cap, with the ends bunched low at the nape of her neck. Her eyes were large and blue under almost straight brows and her features were good. It was a face that could attract a lot of favorable attention except that it had all the warmth and mobility of an iceberg off Greenland. Her dress was billowing black net and it fitted her right, but it was no importation. She held a pencil and a small notebook and was telling Griswold where to put his chips in a quiet voice that belonged with her face.

As far as roulette was concerned they were doing fine. There were stacks of chips and layers of banknotes in front of him—a small mountain of them and growing all the time.

Bets were being placed for the next spin of the wheel. The blonde put sizable stacks on two numbers. Her back was to me and I couldn't see much of her face. But what I could see of the rest of her made it a nice evening. Griswold, on orders from the redhead, shoved three tall piles of green chips on the black diamond, his hands shaking slightly. There were other chips on the board but they didn't matter to the crowd. The attention was all on the Griswolds.

The croupier was a small round man in white tie and tails. His expression was sad and a little worried, as if all house losses came out of his weekly pay check. This not being Monte Carlo or an Oppenheim novel, he used his hands to handle the chips instead of one of those wooden rakes you see in pictures. He gave the layout a jaundiced once-over, spun the wheel and with a practiced flip of the wrist sent the ivory ball around the groove in the opposite direction.

I slid a hand in my pocket and got out my slender supply of money and eased up to the board, between the blonde Mrs. Griswold and the lean slice of manhood known to me as Mr. Smith. The blonde was too busy watching the skittering ivory marble even to turn her head. Smith gave me an annoyed glance, looked away, then jerked his eyes back to me. The color ran out of his cheeks like water down the drain. His face turned to stone and fury darkened his blue eyes.

"Greetings," I said smugly. "You haven't got that two hundred bucks handy, have you?"

He made a rough, whispering sound deep in his throat. He couldn't stop looking at me. The hand holding the highball jerked just enough to slop some of the contents over the rim.

A murmur from the crowd caught my attention. The marble was out of the groove and bouncing musically along the metal slots. It settled suddenly in one of them with a sharp click and stuck there, riding it until the wheel stopped.

"Black Thirteen," the croupier announced evenly. No one was on the number. He matched Griswold's chips on the black diamond and swept the rest of the board clean.

The redhead consulted her notebook with an aloof calmness. "Sixteen and nineteen, *à cheval,*" she murmured.

The blonde said, "Oh, for God's sake!" in a cool throaty way and pushed half the balance of her chips violently onto the square containing the red diamond. "You sure you didn't rig this wheel, Jules? Or do I have to ride with my husband just to win a few stinking dollars?"

Griswold was stacking his winnings. He said, "Why not try it once, Eve?" He sounded pleasant in an absent-minded way. "Without a system you're just throwing money away."

Eve Griswold snatched up her highball and took a long pull at the liquor with a kind of insolent grace. She put the glass down on the table with a thump and drawled, "I hadn't realized we were so hard pressed, darling. I could always take in washing."

The words were said loud enough to be heard clear back

to the fringe of the crowd. Lawrence Griswold flushed solidly and his hands were suddenly still on the chips in front of him. The sharp hiss of an indrawn breath was Smith's reaction to Eve Griswold's lack of manners.

"Place your bets, please," the croupier said indifferently. Bad manners and short tempers were an old story to him.

I worked a couple of dollar bills from my wallet and leaned past Eve Griswold to drop them next to her chips on the red diamond. My shoulder brushed against her, letting her know I was there. She turned her head without haste and looked me full in the face.

"I might end up giving you a hand with that washing," I said.

She stared at me out of dark-blue eyes with their own brand of casual arrogance. She was as lovely as they come and she had known it long enough to stop thinking about it. Under the harsh light her soft gold hair had a hot look but the face below it seemed cool enough. The small firm chin would take a lot of licks without screaming for help; and while the thin high line of her nose suggested a quick temper, the mouth would smile without much effort.

Hardly any smile this time, though. Not much more than a stirring at the corners of lips that were neither full nor thin but wholly desirable. Dark brows that were more than penciled lines lifted with faint interest—the kind of faint interest that, under the proper circumstances, might get some meat on its bones.

"Aren't you overdoing it a little?" she asked negligently.

"It's only money, Mrs. Griswold."

"That's not what I meant."

"I was afraid it wasn't."

We were being stared at. Griswold's lips were stiff in a chilly half-smile; and while Smith was out of my range at the moment, his eyes would be poison-tipped dirks. The redhead was deep in her notebook; as far as she was concerned I was out to lunch.

The ivory ball whirred like a sleepy rattler . . . and conditions were back to normal. I watched it slip out of the groove and rattle along the tines. It fell into the green double zero and was still there while the layout was being swept clean.

"Pardon me," I said ruefully, "while I step out in the rose garden and shoot myself."

Her smile was all I had hoped it would be. "Well, don't bleed on the rhododendrons. The management would never forgive you."

"Come to think of it," I said, "I'd better not. I've got a date at one o'clock."

Lawrence Griswold had lost even his half-smile. "You might introduce your friend, Eve," he said with a casualness that wasn't casual at all.

A voice next to me said, "My fault, Larry. This is Paul Pine; Mr. and Mrs. Griswold."

I said, "Thanks, Stu," without looking at him. "Not that I meant to push in," I said, looking into Eve Griswold's eyes. They were eyes deep enough for the high-dive board and as blue as distant mountains under a summer haze. "But there are times when Stu's a little slow with introductions."

"Place your bets, please," the croupier said patiently.

Griswold clicked a pile of chips as a polite hint that I was holding up his fun. I said, "Go right ahead. I've already passed my limit. Nice meeting you. Maybe I'll stop in for a drink the next time I'm out your way."

"Do that," Lawrence Griswold said. He might even have meant it.

Eve Griswold said nothing. She was watching me, a spark of laughter far back in her deep eyes, and fumbling with the jeweled clasp of a sequined bag I hadn't noticed before. Likely it was crammed with thousand-dollar bills. I grinned at her and said, "Don't feel bad about my losing. A man in my line makes millions."

I turned away, meeting the white strained face of the man who called himself Smith. I flapped the back of a hand lightly against one of his forearms in a comradely gesture as I went by, said, "See you around, Stu," and pushed through the crowd and headed toward the stairs leading to the ground floor.

CHAPTER 17

It was a clear cool night, almost cold in fact, with the smell of autumn prematurely in the air and a full white moon riding the distant sky. I passed the Loop at a few minutes past eleven and drove north through Lincoln Park, its trees and bushes cold and lonely under the wind and the moon, and beyond them the dull pound of lake surf as ominous as distant artillery.

At Pratt Boulevard I drove west to Wayne Avenue and along it until I found parking space a quarter of a block south of the Dinsmore Arms. I resisted the wind long enough to wrestle my bags out of the boot and lugged them over to the building entrance, fought the door open and went in.

The lobby lights were out at this hour. At the far end Sam Wilson, the nightman, sat at the switchboard, his head hanging over the pages of a pulp magazine. It was the last touch needed to put me where I had left off five days before.

He got out of the chair to welcome me. "Hi there, Mr. Pine! I thought you was away on a vacation."

I put down the bags and leaned against the counter and looked at him. He was as fat and as sloppy and as nosey as ever. His cloudy eyes squinted at me through thick lenses bridging a shapeless nose. Dandruff sprinkled the shoulders of his dark coat, like salt on licorice. His last shave had been as careless as all those before it and his teeth still cried for the brush. But he was part of being home and I almost reached out to pat him on the head.

"I broke one of my skis," I said. I pointed at the magazine he was holding. "How's it going?"

He let me see the cover. It showed, in colors that screamed, a man on the floor with a knife in his chest. A blonde with a topheavy bosom and hardly any nightgown was crouched over him staring at her hand. There was blood on her fingers and it bothered her. It bothered me, too. Maybe next time she'd be more careful.

"One of them society capers," Sam said, tasting the words. "This here private eye is trying to get the girl off the spot, y'see, because he's pretty sure she ain't killed nobody. But the cops think different and he's hiding her out in his apartment. And all along she's got the——"

"I'll read it," I said. "The minute you finish, I'll read it. A guy in my line can't know too much. Any mail or messages?"

He came reluctantly back from a world where murder was fun and went over to the rack to see. He gave me three phone messages that were from the social side of my life. I shoved them in a pocket and gathered up the two pieces of battered luggage and a morning paper off the pile on the counter and got into the self-service elevator. Sam was back in his magazine before I pushed the button.

I unlocked the door to 307 and dropped the bags inside and flipped up the wall switch, lighting the end-table lamps flanking the blue-and-beige-striped davenport across the room. Home never looked better. The hotel maids had taken advantage of my absence to put in some extra licks. The air was a little close but opening a window would fix that.

I threw my hat on the blue lounge chair and went into the kitchen to put water and the right amount of coffee in the percolator and lighted the gas under it. There was half a bottle of Scotch in the cupboard. I got it down and drank a hooker, neat, to hold me together while I unpacked my bags and stored them back in the bedroom closet to gather dust.

By the time that was done the aroma of coffee filled the apartment. I sat at the kitchen table and drank three cups—black and laced with molasses rum—over the morning paper, reading Dick Tracy for information and the editorial page for laughs. I was in the middle of an article that pointed out the Republican Party was not dead but sleeping, when the phone rang in the living room.

It was Sam Wilson, at the desk. "Lady down here wants to come up, Mr. Pine." He sounded faintly outraged. "I told her you just got in and was tired, but she——"

"Who asked you?" I growled. "She give her name?"

A silence while he put a grubby paw over the mouthpiece to ask her. "A Miss Pinkerton, Mr. Pine."

It sprung my jaw for a couple of seconds, then I got it. "Okay." I sighed. "Tell her to come up."

I opened the door while she was coming down the hall. She was wearing a party dress under a soft gray-fur stole and she had done something with her hair that got my red corpuscles out of bed in a hurry.

"Pinkerton!" I growled, letting her in. "Next thing you'll be wearing a deerstalker hat and carrying an enlarging glass. Partner!"

Susan Griswold let the wrap slide from her shoulders and dropped it across the lounge chair. "Nice," she murmured, surveying the room. "I thought private detectives lived in one room and hung their socks on the radiator to dry."

"They let me do janitor work to pay the rent," I said. "Sit down; you can stay long enough to have one drink."

She was carrying a small bag about the size of a business envelope, that glittered under the light. She sank down on the couch and crossed her legs under the wide skirt of the ankle-length moss-green dress and took out a cigarette case in white gold and a lighter in the same metal.

"I saw you there tonight," she said matter-of-factly. "You did all right, too. You must crash a lot of parties with that technique."

"Yeah," I agreed. "I'm real cute. Scotch or Irish?"

Her forehead wrinkled. She looked about sixteen, dressed for her first ball. "Who?"

"Not who," I said, sighing. "Which? Scotch whisky or Irish whisky?"

She considered the question as though it was important. "Scotch, I guess. Not too strong, please. Liquor makes me unpredictable."

"You don't need liquor for that. Not you. Sit still."

I returned to the kitchen and gulped down the rest of the coffee in my cup and made a couple of plain-water highballs and carried them back into the other room. Susan Griswold was standing at the window, the blind up, smoking her cigarette and looking down into Wayne Avenue. She came back to the couch, sampled the drink I handed her and wrinkled her nose. "I'll never really like to drink," she said.

I looked at my strap watch. Eleven-forty. "How did you find me?" I asked, sitting down next to her and putting my heels on the edge of the cocktail table.

"I—I tailed you. Isn't that what it's called?"

"I'll be damned! And I never suspected a thing!"

She dimpled. "You're kind of disappointing as a detective. I wasn't ten feet away from you while you were getting your hat at the checkroom out there. You seemed awfully grim about something. You look quite handsome when you're grim."

"Tut-tut. I was thinking." I looked at the bare, gracefully rounded arm next to me. It had a few freckles and a platinum wrist watch about the size of a dime set in a bracelet only money could buy. "What were you doing out there?"

"Oh, I had a date. Dave Chalmers took me but he passed out. He always does. I sent him home in a cab."

"Who's Dave Chalmers?"

"They live across the road from us. He's nice except when he drinks too much—which is most of the time. Why are we talking about him?"

"Search me." I beat down an impulse to pat that nice rounded arm and hoisted my glass and drank. She watched me gravely, even a little disapprovingly. I said, "That's quite a stepmother you got there, Miss Griswold. We hit it off fine."

"Don't feel so good about it," she said witheringly. "The line forms on the left."

"I'm surprised at you," I said, pained. "A nice girl talking like that."

"Oh, be still!" she snapped. "I'm not a child."

She sucked on her cigarette and blew twin streamers of smoke from her freckled nose to prove it. I chewed back a smile and stretched my legs and listened to the wind take a two-fisted smack at the window. I said, "You still haven't told me what you were doing out there. Or was it your date's idea?"

"Mine," she confessed. "I knew Father and Eve were going. I wanted to keep an eye on him."

"A wasted evening, huh? Outside of one remark she made, they seemed to get along all right."

"That's where you're wrong." Her expression was troubled now and I suddenly realized it had been troubled all along despite her efforts at covering up with a pretense at light chatter. "Right after you left they got into some kind of argument and she flounced out. I suppose she took a cab and went home. Father was pretty much upset. He evidently told Miss Abbott she could go, too, because Mr. Whitney and she left a couple of minutes later."

"And," I said, "you walked out and left your poor old father all alone in that den of iniquity. Weren't you afraid another blonde might get him?"

She bit down on her teeth and I thought she was going to heave the glass at me. "You don't believe me, do you?" she grated. "You think I'm just a busybody or afraid he'll leave all his money to her. What do I have to do to convince you it's not that way at all? What do I have to do to prove I l-love my father and I can't just stand idly by and let her—?"

"Okay, okay," I said hastily. "You're going to save him from himself and I think it's admirable. You may be misguided but you sound sincere. Only, where do I come in?"

She gulped from her glass and leaned over to set it on the table near my feet. Some of the angry color left her face. "I told you why, on the telephone earlier this evening. You're trying to find out something about Eve yourself. I told you how I know that, and when you asked me for a picture of her I was sure. We both want the same thing—that's why I said we should work together."

"Maybe we don't," I said. "As far as I'm concerned she may be exactly what she claims to be—a former canary named Eve Shelby who managed to take advantage of our American way of life by marrying a millionaire. If it turns out that way my interest in her ceases abruptly."

"And if she's somebody else—the somebody you think she might be—then what?"

I shrugged. "She might be either one of two different people. In case she's number one I'll tell my client where to reach her—as I was hired to do. If she's number two I'll ask her where I can find number one. I hope that's clear to you. It is to me."

"And that's as far as you'll go, is that it?" she demanded icily. "Even if she's the one who murdered Mary Conrad and this other girl you mentioned on the phone?"

I swished the contents of my glass in a small whirlpool, getting a musical note from the ice cubes. "Why not make up your mind, Miss Griswold? When I tried to sell you on the idea of tossing her to the buttons this afternoon you almost blew a fuse. Now you're bawling me out for letting her get away with it."

"When I bawl you out you'll know it," she said hotly. "Father would put every nickel he's got into getting her off if she was accused now. We've got to get such complete proof that he *knows* what she is. *Then* we can go to the police."

"And why will I help you get the proof?"

Her eyes got very wide. "Well, my goodness, you're a detective, aren't you?"

"Not that kind of a detective. Murders are police business and they kick the lungs out of anyone who gets in their way. I wasn't hired to dabble in a murder case and I'm not going to be hired to. Not even by you."

"It seems to me you're in one whether you like it or not!"

I blew out my breath. "I'm not in over my head, if that's what you mean. It's not a question of solving the case to keep the law off my own neck. That's happened a couple of times to me in the past and I didn't like it. Not at all, Miss Griswold, believe me."

She eyed me narrowly, thought of something and played it as a trump. "What if I should tell the police you let me leave Mary Conrad's apartment this afternoon? That would put them on your neck!"

"It would bruise yours a little, too," I pointed out. "Don't get out of your depth on this business, Miss Griswold. If your stepmother is as bad as you're trying to make out, she'll slip up one of these days and you'll have her."

While she was picking up her glass I took a quick glance at my wrist watch. I still had time for a shower and a change of clothing, provided I could get Susan Griswold out the door sometime during the next fifteen minutes or so.

I swallowed some more of my highball and watched her watch me. Finally I said, "If you want to help me find out what I want to know about Eve Shelby Griswold, that's fine. But I won't promise to give you the facts about her if I manage to get them. If she's killed somebody and the proof is thrust into my hot little hand, then the cops are going to get it. Not on your account but because I don't cover up for murderers. If you're interested in that kind of one-sided deal, well and good and you're in the firm and can sit behind my office desk on Easter Sundays. But if what I learn about her indicates that her mistakes are minor and in the past, provided there are any mistakes to begin with, then you'll go your way and I'll go mine. Period. That's the contract I'm offering you. Sign it or tear it up and go home so I can get to bed."

She rubbed the edge of her glass slowly back and forth against the point of her chin, her eyes distant, thinking over my offer. Presently she moved her shoulders in a faint shrug. "If that's the way it's got to be . . . all right."

I finished my drink and stood up. "Can I freshen your glass?"

She shook her head. I went back to the kitchen and refilled my order. When I got back she was lighting a fresh cigarette with the stub of the old. I dropped down beside her and put my head back and stared at the ceiling.

"This Whitney you mentioned," I said dreamily. "Stu Whitney, isn't it?"

"That's right. He's the man I mentioned while we were at Mary Conrad's apartment this afternoon."

"What's her interest in him? Or is it the other way around?"

She stirred slightly, bringing her shoulder against mine. Barely touching, but I was aware of it being there. "Both, I think," she said quietly. "I don't know much about him except he's always underfoot. He made a play for me right after Eve brought him into the family."

I grinned. "How did he make out?"

"How do you think?" She sniffed. "He reminds me of something that's crawled out of an abandoned oil well."

"Seems to have plenty of money."

"Well, don't ask me where he gets it. Not honestly, if I know anything."

I took a pull at my Scotch. "You must know *something* about him if he's around all the time."

"Well, he's got an apartment at the Barryshire," she said. "That snooty apartment building on Barry, just off Sheridan Road. I've never gone there and I don't intend to."

I said, "Your stepmother and Whitney just friends, or does he hold her hand when Pop's not looking?"

"I'm sure I wouldn't know," she said stiffly. "If there's anything like that between them, they manage to keep it a deep secret. Matter of fact," she added thoughtfully, "I've seen her draw away when he happened to brush against her."

I looked down at her arm where it touched mine. "You mean even casually, like this?"

Susan Griswold met my eyes but she did not draw away. Her lips twitched in what could be a smile if somebody insisted. "You think you're tough," she murmured. "Hard and fast and funny. Especially funny. Like the end man in a burlesque show!"

"You mean a minstrel show," I said.

She wasn't listening. We went on staring into each other's

eyes. Hers were darker now and very lovely. She didn't mention how mine looked. Her lips were parted slightly. The light shone on them. The low-cut bodice of her evening dress moved unevenly. I leaned down and kissed her. Her lips were cool and not surprised—and then they were warm and clinging and one of her hands moved up and slid softly across the back of my neck.

You never know how long it lasts. She pulled away almost violently and some of her drink spilled on the rug. She slumped back against the upholstery and caught her lower lip with her teeth and didn't look at me. Outside, the wind whimpered and the trees rustled their leaves like the whisper of many voices.

She said clearly, "That didn't mean a thing. I hope you know that."

"Sure."

"I invited it and I got it. I don't know why I invited it and it won't happen again. Please remember that."

"Sure."

Her head jerked around and she glared at me. "Oh, go to hell!"

Abruptly we were laughing. She put down her glass and got a handkerchief from her bag and dried her hand where some of the drink had splashed. She said, "You're crazy but I like you. Now that we've made a deal and I've had my kiss, I'd better be running along."

She took a final drag at her cigarette and rubbed it out and stood up. I went over to the door with her and reached for the knob. She laid a cool palm on the back of my hand, stopping me.

"I think they're up to something, Paul," she said tensely. "My stepmother, Stuart Whitney, Ruth Abbott. I think they know what you're trying to do and they're scared. I could see it in their faces just before they left the Tropicabana."

"Don't start imagining things. Who is this Ruth Abbott?"

"I told you about her. Eve's frozen-faced social secretary. I think she's in love with Stu Whitney. Serve them both right if she is!"

"How you talk!"

She took away her hand and I opened the door. She moved past me, the soft gray fur of her wrap brushing my arm, then turned quickly and pulled my head down. Her lips hadn't cooled any. I reached for her but she slipped away, leaving me with the door.

"Good night, Paul," she breathed.

The elevator door clanged and she was gone. I closed the door and took the glasses into the kitchen and rinsed them out along with my coffee cup and the percolator. While I was putting them in the cupboard I caught the reflection of my face in the glass. The silly grin on it belonged to me.

I got out my handkerchief and wiped my lips and stared at the lipstick smears. Susan Griswold's lipstick. I wondered what I had done to deserve it.

CHAPTER 18

THE WIND was still at it. Nothing moved along the walks except shadows. Shadows that swooped and crept and retreated, like ghosts afraid of shadows.

Farwell Avenue, here, was twin rows of small neat apartment buildings, none higher than three floors. I stood in the shadows of a passageway and watched the street. An occasional window showed a glimmer of light but most of them were as black and empty as the lifeless sockets of a skull.

Time passed with dreary reluctance. Only the wind hurried. A tree groaned in the parkway near me and somewhere a loose shutter banged monotonously. I took out a cigarette and rolled it around in my fingers, unlighted, until it fell apart. I pulled the collar of my topcoat higher around my ears. I took off my hat and reshaped the crown and jammed it back on.

Headlights turned the corner at Lakewood Avenue and came slowly east along the street toward me.

It wasn't the Cadillac after all. A Buick sedan this time, and last year's model at that. It passed me and nosed into a parking space a couple of doors farther down, found it too small and backed out again. Another twenty feet and it slid gently along the curb, its two wire parking guides strumming musically against the concrete. The headlights blinked, then died, and almost immediately the parking lights came on.

I shifted my position just enough to keep the car in sight without being seen myself. Both taillights glowed brightly red, like danger signals. The car doors remained closed.

Some time passed. A car went by with a soundless rush and turned into Sheridan Road a block to the east. A tiny flame flickered briefly inside the Buick as a cigarette was lighted. Nothing now but the wind and the shadows and the lights on the waiting car.

Five minutes went by. A gloved hand appeared at the window beside the wheel and dropped the stub of a cigarette into the street. The wind seized it and carried a streamer of sparks into oblivion. I patted the bulge under my left arm and continued to lean against the passageway bricks.

Again a flame came to life inside the car and died quickly. She was on her second cigarette now. She might wait until it had burned down, but no longer than that. She would be impatient and on edge and beginning to doubt.

I drew my hat down to keep it from sailing and stepped out onto the walk. The tree shadows did their best to hide me. I eased over to the curb and along it to the rear of the Buick. Nobody yelled at me, no windows slammed up in any of the buildings, no night sticks drummed against the walks.

I stood near the car's right rear wheel and peered through the glass. She was alone. I could make out her head and shoulders. She was wearing a hat with a heavy veil, like a new widow on her way to the funeral. The lights on the dash were turned off, leaving the interior too dark for me to decide if there was something familiar about her.

Another step and I was able to look at the floor between the seats. Nobody was crouched there with a gun in his teeth. My hand was on the door release before she saw me standing there. She started visibly and shrank back against the opposite door. I tried to open the door and found it locked.

One of her hands moved and the rays of a pencil flash shone on my face through the glass. The light winked out and she leaned over and released the catch.

"You're late," she said throatily, as I slid in beside her and closed the door. "I was about ready to give up on you."

It was like the voice on the phone and yet not like it. Disguised voices are never quite the same twice in a row. She was wearing a black cloth coat with dolman sleeves. Its bulk kept me from making out her size but even so she wasn't a large woman. A checkered scarf puffed out between the lapels of her coat, muffling her neck and chin. Her cigarette glowed softly between the gloved fingers of her left hand where it rested against the wheel.

I drew up one knee and turned on the seat toward her. The interior of the car reeked of smoke. The veil made her face no more than a black blob.

"I'm Grace Rehak," she murmured. "Let's get this over with."

"Okay," I said cheerfully. "Take off the veil and we'll get down to business."

She shrank back in sudden alarm. "No! I told you this was the way it would have to be. Who hired you to find me?"

I got out a cigarette, patted my pockets for a match, then reached for the stub she was holding. She started to hold it out but my hand swerved sharply, grasped her hat and yanked. It and the veil came away. She cried out and covered her face with her gloves.

"Too late, Mrs. O'Flynn," I said mildly.

The hands came down slowly. Her face was white and strained and angry. "So now you know," she said flatly.

"I had an idea to begin with," I said. "So Grace Rehak

is Steven O'Flynn's wife. Why all the secrecy about it?"

"You don't think I could let him know, do you?" she said sullenly. "That I was . . . well, that I worked for Bertha Lund?"

"Oh, hell," I said. "Who do you think hired me?"

She straightened as though I'd struck her. "What! You mean Steve—? That's a lie!"

"What makes you so sure, Mrs. O'Flynn?"

"Why, he knows I——" She stopped abruptly and her eyes slid away from mine.

"Go on," I said softly. "Finish it. He knows you couldn't be Grace Rehak, is that it?"

She moistened her lips. "Why would I say I was her if I wasn't?"

"Why make me point out the obvious?" I said. "You're saying it because the real Grace Rehak hired you to say it. She hired you to make this date before I ever showed up at the Tropicabana tonight. You answered the description Bertha Lund gave me while I was in Lincoln—a description she passed on to Grace Rehak when she called to warn her about me.

"Bertha lied about everything else, so why not this? For all I know Grace could be any size, any shape, any complexion, even a redhead—not like you at all."

She ground her teeth together, saying nothing.

"Let me dress it up a little more for you," I went on. "Yesterday afternoon your Mr. Smith, or Stuart Whitney, tried to buy the name of my client from me. He's tied up with Gracie some way. Just tonight I saw him at the Tropicabana with two dames, a blonde and a redhead. Either one might have been her.

"When I told him I'd do my talking only to Grace Rehak,

and in person, let's just for the hell of it say he passed the word on to her and between them they cooked up this idea of you subbing for her long enough to find out what I want. It makes sense too, for if Gracie is that afraid of being found out, she wouldn't come within a mile of me for *any* reason."

"If you knew that," she sneered, "why bother to show up here tonight at all?"

"To learn who the real Grace Rehak is these days."

She dropped the remains of her cigarette to the floor boards and set a foot on it. "I told you I'm Grace Rehak. If you don't want to believe it then take the air. I'm not going to sit here all night and chin with you."

"You're going to tell me how to go about finding her, Mrs. O'Flynn."

Silence while the wind tried to kick in the windshield. She was staring at me blankly.

"You're going to tell me," I went on, "or you're going to find yourself up to your permanent wave in a murder rap. Mary Conrad was killed because she knew the name Gracie is using. You know it too—otherwise Grace Rehak wouldn't have given you enough information to make your impersonation of her stand up with me. A woman killed Mary Conrad. I don't think Grace Rehak did the job as long as she could hire somebody else to do it, and since she hired you to meet me she could have hired you to do the job on Mary. At least that's the story I give to the cops unless you see things my way."

She reached for the black-leather bag in her lap but my hand was there first. I couldn't feel the outlines of a gun. She said, "I want a cigarette."

"Go ahead." I handed the bag to her and she got out a case and took out one of its cork-tipped contents. I struck a match for her and she straightened up and pushed the bag down between her and the door and brought up a pearl-handled belly gun and pointed it at me.

"Move back," she said between her teeth. "And keep your hands on your knees."

This was something I hadn't expected. This made no sense at all. I inched away from her, as ordered, and kept on looking at the gun. I said, "This is crazy. What're you trying to buy with that?"

"Maybe I'm going to kill you," she said sardonically. "If I could have killed Mary Conrad why couldn't I give you the same?"

"As stupid as you are," I said around my thick tongue, "you're not that stupid. Killing me will only force my client to put a new man on Gracie's trail. You can't expect to go on doing it. Even Gracie knows that."

She said nothing. She reached out and fumbled at the dashboard. The headlights blinked on and off, once. "All right," she said coldly. "You'll talk to her. But keep your eyes straight ahead. Try turning your head an inch either way and I'll shoot your leg off!"

I heard the rear door of the Buick open slowly behind me. The hair crawled along my scalp. The door clicked shut and there was the rustle of a movement at my back. A hand rested lightly on my right shoulder and slid carefully down under the lapels of my coat. Fingers closed about the butt of my gun, freed it from the holster and came out with it. I looked down my nose. It was a woman's hand, strong and capable, light glinting on the painted nails. The gun disappeared behind me.

I waited, having trouble with my breathing. The sound of a sharply indrawn breath was my only warning. I jerked my head aside just as a truck rolled across one side of it with a clashing of gears. Agony poured in, blinding me. My reflexes twisted me up and around and I lunged at her. One of my hands struck against a firm breast, closed there and tried to tear it out by the roots.

I never had a chance. A second blow knocked me away. It wasn't a glancing blow this time and it finished the job. The world jarred and turned into darkness filled with silent explosions of light that fell in a long slow curve into a shoreless sea.

And, as slowly, I fell with them.

CHAPTER 19

SOMEBODY had shoved a pillow under my face. Not the most comfortable pillow you could find; it was too firm and there was a long narrow hollow running the length of it. There was a very faint odor of what seemed to be bath salts, if that was possible.

My head buzzed like a bee hive. Pain was everywhere; the universe was filled with pain and my head was the center of the universe. I lay very still and waited for the coroner to arrive. I thought about finding a phone and calling him myself, only that's no job for a corpse. Let somebody else do it, like always.

Slowly it all came back to me. I didn't move. Good old Pine. One of the smart movie-type private boys. Tough as a millionaire's surtax and always smart. Smart enough to make a date with a killer and expect to keep out of trouble doing it.

I pushed myself up off the car seat and lay back panting, not opening my eyes. The smell of bath salts was gone now, and in its place was an acrid, biting odor. I knew that smell and my teeth clicked shut and my eyes opened.

She was still there, sitting behind the wheel, her head leaning against the window, a hand resting on either side of her against the seat. She did not move. She would never move again. She was dead.

A thin dark line along the side of her neck was a tracing of blood. I gritted my teeth and leaned sideways and parted the hair around her ear. The bullet had made a nice clean hole in the bulge of occipital bone there. She had died instantly, without pain and without fear.

I slid away from her and started to reach for the door handle on my side of the Buick. My foot struck against something on the floor boards and I glanced down. It was a gun. My gun. A lot of good it had done me tonight. I might as well have brought along one that fired caps.

I bent and picked it up, getting a sharp shooting pain across the back of my head as a reward. I placed the muzzle to my nose and sniffed. It reeked of freshly burned powder fumes.

My face got as stiff as an ice floe. What had started out as a vague suspicion was now cold realization. Bonnie O'Flynn had died from a bullet fired from my gun.

I sat there while my stomach turned into a hard core of fear. Susan Griswold was right after all. I was in over my head now. It was a case of unraveling the knot or being hanged with it.

I had to know something first. I took hold of Bonnie O'Flynn's head and turned it. It turned easily; the flesh was still warm and rigor mortis not yet moving in. I carefully examined every inch of her head, running my fingers lightly over her scalp.

No exit wound anywhere. That meant the bullet from my .38 Colt Detective Special was still in there. It might be too badly flattened for ballistics purposes, but I couldn't count on it.

Her purse was still shoved down next to her on the seat. I took out my handkerchief, covered my fingers with it and snaked the purse out into the open. Nothing in it that wasn't in half the purses in town. But no papers, no clues, nothing I could use to erase the spot I was in.

The bag went back where I found it. Very carefully I

wiped every surface I might have touched, awake or unconscious. That might remove the killer's prints as well as my own but that wasn't important now.

I struck a match and looked at my wrist watch. One-forty. I had been sleeping in Bonnie O'Flynn's lap something like twenty-five or thirty minutes. A killer could get far in that much time. Maybe even as far as Lake Ridge, the swank North Shore suburb, if she hurried. Or was I kidding myself?

The street was still deserted, the wind still howled, shadows continued to weave and shiver along walks and parkways. Hardly any lighted windows now. Bonnie O'Flynn sat stiff and still, as quiet as the death that filled her, her white face glistening, her hat with its veil on the floor between her feet. I looked at the keys in the ignition and thought of driving the Buick and its cargo to some quiet street far from my hotel. It wouldn't do anything for me and it might snap back in my face. If the bullet in Bonnie O'Flynn could be made to match my gun, I was caught by the short hairs; if not, they could find the car parked in my hotel lobby and I could still thumb my nose at them.

The car door opened easily under my hand. I backed out unsteadily, my right hand around the gun butt in the pocket of my topcoat. Not that I would shoot anybody; it gave me a comfortable feeling to hold onto something stronger than I was right then.

I walked slowly west along Farwell, reeling slightly like a delegate to the wine-tasters' convention. The wind felt wonderful against my head but there was a dull ache across the top of it that a bucket of aspirins would never dent.

As I turned into Wayne Avenue a car hit me with its headlights. I lowered my head and plodded on and the car went on by, trailing swing-band music from its radio.

I continued on past the entrance to the Dinsmore Arms, trying not to think of the empty bed in 307. I fished out my keys and unlocked the Plymouth and managed to crawl in. My fingers were shaking when I switched on the ignition. I leaned down across the wheel, feeling the sweat stand out on my forehead and cheeks.

It passed. By the time I was turning south into Sheridan Road I was ready for anything less strenuous than brushing my teeth.

The Barryshire was twelve floors of granite and glass a hundred feet west of Sheridan Road, on Barry Avenue. It had a leaded-glass canopy, a double line of toy hedges on either side of the entrance walk, and the elegant air of a dowager lifting a teacup. The rest of the street was on much the same scale, lined with apartment buildings that were large and modern and high in the rents. Four blocks to a yacht harbor, in case you had a yacht. Plenty of street lamps to discourage purse-snatchers and footpads. Even the wind seemed to walk softly along it.

Only a few blocks from where Mary Conrad had died, yet worlds apart otherwise. I wondered if being that close meant anything.

Halfway down the block I found a parking place. While I was getting out, a couple crossed the walk from one of the entrances and got into a car big enough to hold the Jukes family. It pulled away from the curb and rolled past me toward Broadway, its motor as quiet as butterflies wrestling.

I pushed open the heavy door to the Barryshire and went in. The foyer was large and brilliantly lighted. The floor was gray-asphalt tiling, the walls dark blue, the arched ceiling painted white. A line of recessed mailboxes were set in each of the side walls. Farther back, close to an inner door of glass squares, were twin rows of bell buttons next to a house phone in an arched niche.

Midway down one row I found a neat black name plate with gold letters that read STUART WHITNEY—5B. I stared at it thoughtfully for what seemed a long time. I poised a finger over the button, lowered it before doing anything rash, and went over and tried the inner door. It was locked. I hadn't expected it not to be. I came back and stared at the name plate some more. It hadn't changed any. Make up your steel-trap mind, Pine.

I set the ball of a thumb against the gilt button opposite Stuart Whitney's name, holding it there longer than good manners would dictate. Then I took it away and picked up the house phone.

He was already at the other end. "Yes? Who is it?" The words were quick, almost breathless, the voice light and husky.

"Paul Pine, Mr. Smith. Remember?"

Silence from the other end. If he had fainted I didn't hear the body fall. Nothing clicked against my ear, so the connection was still open. I said, "Want to talk to you. Press the buzzer; it's drafty down here."

More silence came back to me. I opened my mouth to drive home the idea, but the click that hadn't come before came now. He had hung up on me. I was reaching out to stab the button a second time when the lock on the inner door began to rattle.

Beyond it were a flight of gray carpeted steps and the door to an elevator. I brought down the self-service cage and rode up to the fifth floor surrounded by enough chrome and mirrors to outfit a cocktail bar. The corridor was wide, clean and lighted by soft amber bulbs. Doors with gilt numbers mounted on small heraldic shields lined both sides.

5B was all the way back and around a corner. Just as I reached it, the door opened silently and Stuart Whitney stood looking out at me.

He was as handsome, as clean-shaved and as supercillious

as I remembered. He was wearing a loose-fitting blue brocaded silk robe drawn together almost to his chin, the belt knotted tightly in a double loop. The legs of maroon pajamas were visible below the robe, with bare ankles and brown leather slippers below those.

If hearing my name over the house phone had upset him, it no longer showed in his expression. He surveyed me coolly past the edge of the door. "I suppose I should have expected something like this. Your profession must call for a certain amount of cunning."

My grin was a smirk. "You have no idea how easy it was. Am I coming in?"

He let me see that he was making up his mind about it. Finally he stepped back and drew open the door wide enough for me to sidle through. I went past him and looked at a long, rather narrow living room worth coming a long way to see. It was alive with harsh contrasting colors that at first glance clashed like a bucket of bolts through a plate-glass window.

The all-over carpeting was a deep coral broadloom, three of the walls were a dull deep green and the fourth a very pale gray, the ceiling a pastel blue. The furniture was blond oak and as severe in the lines as a cube of sugar. Against one of the green walls was an oversize sofa covered with a rough material in chartreuse, and in front of the sofa a coffee table slightly smaller than a skating rink.

Two doors, white and closed, in the gray wall would lead into a bedroom and a kitchen. I walked down the room to its one window, a huge low-silled affair framed in raw red silk, and dropped my battered hat on a lamp table that came closer to resembling a veneered packing case than anything else. While I was shrugging out of my topcoat, Whitney closed the door and leaned an elbow negligently against the top of a blond spinet piano I hadn't noticed before.

"No point in getting too comfortable," he said disagreeably. "You're not going to be here that long."

I was still holding the cigarette I had lighted on my way up in the elevator. I looked around for an ash tray. There was a triangular-shaped bowl in glazed ebony next to my hat. My head was beginning to reel a little. I put some ash in the bowl and said, "I should have brought along a piece of smoked glass. What do you sleep on—a rainbow?"

He took his elbow off the piano and let the hand slip into the single pocket of his robe. I didn't think he had a gun in there. He spoke through his teeth. "It's two in the morning in case you don't know it. Say what's to be said and get out. I'm in no mood for your wit."

I drew an armchair covered with gray tapestry nearer to the table and sat in it. "No more wit. That's a promise. When did you get in?"

He stared thoughtfully at me. "What makes that your business? And let me tell you something else. I resent the way you pushed in on the Griswolds tonight, forcing me into introducing you to prevent a scene. You and I have nothing for each other, Pine. I made the mistake of trying to help a friend by seeing you. That's as far as it goes. From now on keep the hell away from me and from the people I know. I mean it."

"Does that include Bonnie Field?"

His face went slowly blank. "So you know about her." He cleared his throat. "I know many people, including Steve O'Flynn and his wife. Why bring her into it?"

"Why not? Isn't she the friend you were trying to help?"

He let the question sink in, trying to decide the best way to answer it. "You mean Grace Rehak?" he said carefully.

"There's reason to think so," I said. "When you came to my office yesterday and tried to learn what my interest was in Grace Rehak, you arrived in her car and it picked you up afterward. Bonnie O'Flynn was at the wheel both times. She fits the description I have of Grace Rehak. Bonnie is married to a successful gambler and night-club owner—a man who might kick her out if he learned she was a former bawdy-house inmate. You see how it adds up, Mr. Whitney?"

Muscles crawled along the slope of his jaw and the sharp edges of his mouth came together. He crossed abruptly to the couch and dropped onto it. A hand came up and drew the already drawn folds of brocaded silk closer about his neck.

"Actually," he said, selecting his words like a housewife squeezing the tomatoes at the corner market, "it adds up to very little. Let's say I happened to have lunch with Mrs. O'Flynn yesterday and casually mentioned I had a call to make on Jackson Boulevard. Since she was driving, what could be more natural than for her to drop me off at your office and pick me up there later?"

"Uh-hunh. And that's what happened?"

He shrugged. "And that's what happened."

"The two of you spend the rest of the afternoon together?"

"Why . . . no. She drove me directly home. Here."

"Did she come up for a while?"

His chin jerked up. "See here, are you hinting——?"

"No hints," I said. "We're both men of the world. Did she or didn't she?"

"She did not! Both the O'Flynns happen to be my very good——"

"It's okay," I said wearily. "I believe you. For my money she was as queer as a square bowling ball. A man was something to pay the bills but useless other than that."

He had flushed clear to the eyebrows. "Queer? Not—?"

"Yeah. Lesbo queer. There are such people. At one time she was mixed up with a crowd of them. Mary Conrad, Ellen

Purcell, Laura Fremont. Even Grace Rehak—only I don't think she was one of them in that respect. Not a girl in her former line of work."

His face was still red. "You've got a nasty mind!" he said almost primly.

"Hunh-uh. I just come up against some nasty people. And not from choice." I straightened out my legs and stared at the brown leather of my shoes, resting my eyes. The ache in my head pulsed in tempo with my heart.

When I glanced up again he was lighting a cigarette with a dull silver table lighter from an angular end table alongside the couch. His hand was shaking a little.

"Anyway," I said, "she let you out in front of the Barryshire and you came up and called Grace Rehak and told her I wouldn't play ball unless I could do the pitching. Is that it?"

"Something like that," he said quietly. "I did pass along your suggestion that she meet you personally."

"How did she take to it?"

"I don't know. The subject was changed."

I looked away from him. There was a very thin line of light under one of the two doors in the gray wall. I could see it because the thick carpeting ended just short of the sill and the heavy pile threw a shadow against the bottom crack. The line of light was not an unbroken line. Something was blocking a section of it from the other side—something that moved slightly as I watched, was still, moved again.

I turned my head to drop my cigarette into the three-cornered bowl. I said, "Well-l-l," without meaning and stood up and shoved my hands loosely into my trouser pockets. I strolled over to the gray wall and studied two large paintings hanging there in blond-wood frames. Impressionistic as all get out. But they went with the rest of the room—if anything could be said to go with it.

When I moved again, I moved fast. The doorknob was turning under my hand before Whitney could get off the couch. I slammed my shoulder against the panel and the door flew back no more than a foot before it hit something soft.

A woman screamed—not loudly, more in surprise than anything else—and the door opened all the way. She was half-crouching, trying to cover everything in sight with her hands and not succeeding. She was wearing a black-net nightgown about half as substantial as the air over Pike's Peak on a clear day. She had red hair and the kind of figure old men use to circulate their blood. She wasn't holding a notebook now.

There was a slight odor of acetone in the air. I said, "My mistake, Miss——"

Fingers grabbed my coat collar from behind and yanked, catching me off balance. I fell back a step and swung the back of my hand and caught Stuart Whitney across one cheek. The fingers fell away from my collar and the husky voice said, "You son of a bitch!" and a set of knuckles crashed squarely against my right eye.

After that it was awhile before anybody moved. Whitney's face was as white as forgiven sins except where the marks of my fingers stood out clearly. The redhead had a white terry-cloth robe around her now. I had missed seeing her put it on.

I straightened my coat and waited a long moment for the pounding in my skull to let up. My eye was already beginning to swell, although the punch it had absorbed was nothing special. I turned my back on my host and his invited guest and trudged over to the lamp table and picked up my hat and listened to the restless wind prowl the street.

When I turned around again Whitney was back on the couch, the lower half of his robe parted and hanging off his legs, his knees together. He took a cigarette from a lacquered box on the coffee table and used the silver lighter, his hands shaking. Ruth Abbott stood straight and tall in the bedroom door, the light glistening along her carmined nails. She stared at me out of glittering eyes, with a cold lack of expression worse than open hatred. The silence was growing as taut as an overdrawn violin string.

"Maybe I had that one coming, Mr. Whitney," I said. "Certainly it's none of my business who you sleep with on a windy night. But finding Grace Rehak is my business and it's time you told me where she is."

He didn't look up. "Get out of here, Pine. Before I throw you out."

"You couldn't throw your weight in Hershey bars," I said. "Listen to me, Whitney. I'm trying to find a girl. Her name is Laura Fremont. I think Grace Rehak can tell me where she is. Neither of those two wants to be found for reasons best known to themselves. Three different girls who knew them both have died of murder to make sure nobody would find at least one of them. So far I don't know which one. But I intend to find out."

Stuart Whitney raised his head slowly. His eyes were a little wild. "You're insane! Murders—what murders?"

"Until tonight," I said, "I was more spectator than anything else. But tonight number three died. She died with my head in her lap, Whitney, and I was to be framed for the job. I would have taken the long step too, only the killer was smart enough to realize it might not end there and that whoever was interested enough in Laura Fremont to hire me could just as easily hire a second private dick to take up where I left off. But now I'm in this all the way. I've got my own neck to save and I mean to save it."

I bent and scooped up my topcoat and hung it over my arm. I walked over and stood in front of him, the coffee table between us. I reached down and took one of the cigarettes out of the lacquered box, shoved it in my face and took the lighter out of his stiff fingers.

"All my leads are gone now," I said. "All except you. From now on your friends are my friends. Among them will be Grace Rehak or Laura Fremont—or both."

I snapped the lighter into flame and got my cigarette burning. I let the flame wink out and bounced the lighter on my palm. "So far," I said, "I know only one of your friends. The blonde babe who likes roulette. Mrs. Eve Shelby Griswold. I kind of like that one. Thirty million bucks and a cloudy background. She'd pay heavy to have you keep her secret, wouldn't she, Whitney? Heavy enough to pay for Brooks Brothers clothing and a technicolor apartment at six hundred a month. No wonder your tongue is nailed!"

I blew out a ribbon of smoke and watched it settle down across the table. The redhead was breathing audibly and unevenly.

"Okay," I said. "I've done a lot of talking—far more than I'm used to. But I'm going to say one thing more. Tell your blonde friend she's next. I'm on to her as of right now. She's going to get backtracked on—all the way back to the day she was conceived. That's it, Whitney. Short and sweet and right in there."

I pitched the lighter into his lap. It went between his legs and bounced along the carpet. I said, "Good night, Miss Abbott. It was nice seeing you."

On the way down in the elevator I looked at the chrome trimmings. They glittered as coldly as Ruth Abbott's eyes.

CHAPTER 20

I WOKE up about ten in a silence that screamed. I sat on the edge of the bed and smoked a cigarette and took inventory of what ailed me. An ache here, a twinge there, a dull pain on top and a burning sensation on the ball of each foot. A man in my line gets used to sore feet.

Outside, the sun was shining and the wind had stopped. That last item would account for the silence. It might even have warmed up. What made that important?

I dragged myself off the bed and crawled into the bathroom. The face in the mirror was a sight for sore eyes. I had a sore eye for the job. Not swollen as much as I thought it would be. Red and a little puffy, but that would go away someday. I put a hand on top of my head and felt the bump there. It seemed a fraction smaller and I could touch it without my knees turning to water.

After a shave and a hot shower I padded into the kitchen and got the coffee going and plugged in the toaster. While they were warming up I put on my best suit and a clean white shirt and tucked a handkerchief in my breast pocket. My shoes could stand a shine and the hair was getting a little too long around the ears and across the back of my neck.

Breakfast lifted the fog enough to get me thinking again. Thinking was worse than the fog. I must have sounded like Hamlet last night. Hamlet at the Barryshire. Hamlet with three skulls to soliloquize over this time. "Alas, poor Ellen and Mary and Bonnie. I hadn't known them at all."

Don't run it into the ground, brother.

I lighted my second cigarette of the day and drifted into the living room to take my hat and topcoat off the couch where I had dumped them at three in the morning. I hung the coat in the bedroom closet and took the Colt .38 out of its holster and went back to the kitchen with it. I tore it apart and cleaned and oiled the works, using very little oil. The fired cartridge case went into the incinerator shaft and I put a fresh shell in its place.

Later I stood looking out the living-room window. The sun was still there, the sky was blue, the birds made a racket, and people went by dressed for the summertime. Nice day for a drive in the country. Nice day to sit in my office and look down into Jackson Boulevard and wait for the phone to ring or the door to open and bring me a job of keeping my eye on the wedding presents or serving a subpoena or getting the goods on some department-store clerk who was knocking down on the till. Anything that had nothing to do with murder and the cops and a flock of dames who figured nature had the wrong slant on sex.

I sat in the easy chair and tried reading last night's paper. It was the diary of a world out of tune. Crimes between countries and crimes between neighbors. Love nests and houses divided and three men had stuck up a grocery on West Sixty-third. An election year and don't change horses while you're cleaning house.

The paper went across the room and I went back to wearing a strip in the rug. Walk out on this, Pine. Give the whole works to the cops and forget it. What is there to hold you in it? Girls disappear every day in the month. You can't find them all, even if you were hired to. Girls with nice old folks that don't drink or break any laws, who look on tobacco as the devil's weed. Tell the Fremonts their daughter is married to the Rajah of Ragoon and wash your hands of the case.

He had been a nice homespun kid. Probably a girl friend and the vague idea of a four-room house and Sundays next to the radio and a pile of papers on the floor. Only a blackjack had spread his brains over a hotel rug and left him to wait for Gabriel's horn.

I went into the kitchen again. The bottle of Irish whisky was still behind the canned goods on the second shelf. I poured two fingers into a glass and drank most of it. It went down hard and tasted like a farmer's boots after a day in the cow pasture. I never drank at this hour of the day.

The suburban phone book listed six numbers under Lawrence Griswold's name. The gate house. The gardener's cottage. The servant's lodge. The guest house. The stables. No listing for an airport. I copied down the number of the main house and put the book away. Just call up and ask for Mrs. Eve Griswold and tell her to stick around, that a private detective with clean cuffs and alcohol on his breath would be out to ask her if she'd murdered anybody lately. The scullery maid would probably throw me in the lake.

Eleven-forty-seven. I picked up the phone and put it down again before the girl downstairs could answer. I got out the right book and looked up the number of the *Daily News*.

This time I didn't hang up. The society editor was most co-operative. The Lawrence Griswolds? Lovely people. His grandfather had been a world-beater. Founded half the New England textile industry and left it all to his son, who had left it all to *his* son. Fifty million dollars if a dime. And quite a man with the ladies, it seemed. (I got a simper along with that.) Married four times, the last three being tall statuesque blondes. His present wife? Good heavens, man, don't you read the papers? Eve Shelby, a night-club singer. Created quite a stir at the time; I'm surprised you missed it. Her background? Well, to tell you the truth, we don't have much on her. Daughter of an obscure Pittsburgh family. After all, a night-club singer . . . Married late last spring. No, her parents hadn't attended. Reported traveling in Europe at the time.

I was sitting on the bed, holding the phone in my lap, after thanking the editor for her trouble, and scowling at the closed closet door for no reason, when the hall-door buzzer sounded.

It could be anybody. I put the phone back on the night-stand and went into the living room and opened the door wide enough to see who it was.

I stepped back quickly before they could tramp on me on the way in. Captain Blauvelt needed the door open all the way to get his shoulders through. The sergeant known as Les ambled in behind him like a tugboat nudging an ocean liner into the dock. He closed the door and leaned against it.

I backed all the way to the couch. "Come in," I said. "Don't wait to be asked. Of course every man's home is his castle, but this is the waiting room at the Union Station."

Blauvelt grunted and took off his hat and let it hang alongside his leg from two fingers. His yellow eyes saw the room and everything in it including a scuffed spot on the toe of my left shoe.

"Didn't get you up, did we?" he rumbled.

"Matter of fact you did. I was just thinking of getting into my pajamas and running downtown."

He grunted again. "Chipper this morning. Nice place you got. What happened to the eye?"

"I went into a man's apartment without an invitation. The rent is reasonable and the furnishings are mine. And I'm not chipper."

He moved ponderously over to the easy chair and sat

down and put his hat carefully on the floor next to it. The sergeant got off the door and glided over and leaned against the side of the bedroom door, not neglecting to look in there.

"Sit down," Blauvelt said. "Go on; you look tired. Out late, I bet."

I didn't say anything to that. But I did sit down. He got out a briar pipe and a blue tobacco tin and lighted up. He had the look of a man who has arrived for the week end.

"No fooling, Pine. How'd you get that eye?"

"I told you. I wouldn't lie to an officer of the law."

"Not much you wouldn't," he said, without rancor. "Any old time you wouldn't." He puffed on his pipe and surveyed me, dreamy-eyed. Les had gone over to lean against the kitchen doorway. By this time he probably knew how many grains of salt I had on hand.

"I spoke to Lieutenant Overmire about you this morning," Blauvelt said suddenly. "He said you could find your way around by taking short cuts. He said you would work along with the cops if they used a thumbscrew on you. That's what he said."

"He should know."

He blew out a blue cloud of smoke and went on looking comfortable and complacent. After listening to the wind yesterday I couldn't get used to the quiet. Blauvelt said, "I thought I'd come by and kick around that killing you were in on yesterday. All right?"

"A Surf Street floozie?" I said, quoting him. "Somewhere I got the idea you were going to handle that as routine. I was wrong, hunh?"

"Sometimes routine leads to a place where it stops being routine." He jerked his leonine head toward the sergeant at the kitchen door without taking his eyes off me. "Les, there, is a good man, Pine. And a hustler. Takes his job serious.

Something about the Conrad bump-off rang a bell in him after a while. He got to digging through the back files on homicides not yet cleared up. And he found out what he was after."

He stopped there and leaned back and crossed his legs on the second try. I tried to keep an expression of polite boredom where he could see it.

"Seems a girl was killed over in a LaSalle Street walk-up early part of this year," Blauvelt said. "Helen somebody-or-other."

"Ellen, Chief," Les said from the doorway, sounding proud. "Ellen Purcell."

"That was it," Blauvelt said. "What made it important, she was pushed the same way the Conrad dame got it—a stocking around her neck. So Les, on his own time, mind you, went over there and had a word with the landlady. She remembered all about it, clear down to some details she'd forgotten during the original investigation. Reason for that, seems some cop was around in plain clothes earlier the same day talking about it. She said he was kind of a nice-looking man, six feet maybe, good build on him, dark hair parted on the side and a small dent in the bridge of his nose."

"Wearing green socks," I said, "a gold crown on his lower right bicuspid and answering to the name of Pine."

"She forgot to mention them first two," Blauvelt said equably, "but she had the name right. She also said you asked first for a girl name of Fremont—she wasn't sure of the first name until Les asked her if it was Laura. Then she was sure. Said you got interested in the Purcell murder when she told you the girl that did the job was named Louise Fairchild." He pointed the stem of his pipe at me. "Same initials as the Fremont girl—*and* the same description."

I said wearily, "One thing about Les, Captain: he won't stay a sergeant long. Not Les."

"He will if I can swing it," the captain said. "You don't think I'd let loose of him, do you? Tell you something else he come up with out there last night. He found out the Purcell kid worked at a night club. Course you know about that. The old bag told you."

"It took some prying," I said. "I made the sergeant's job easy for him. You might remember that, while you're remembering things."

Blauvelt cupped the pipe bowl in his hand, rubbing it gently, the dreamy look still in his lion's eyes. "The Tropicabana," he rumbled. "Now ain't *that* a honey! The same identical joint where Mary Conrad earned her cakes. And Mary knew Laura Fremont too, the way one pervert knows another. So now it turns out Laura Fremont was living with Ellen Purcell—and I mean living with!—killed her during a lovers' quarrel, let's say, then yesterday gave Conrad the same treatment to keep *her* mouth shut. How do you like it, boy?"

"I'm crazy about it. They'll probably make you Commissioner."

He folded his heavy fingers around his knee and squeezed gently. "Course none of this surprises you none," he said expansively. "You ain't dumb, Pine. You'd hold out on me every time you thought you could get away with it, and you run to a very unbright line of chatter. But you ain't dumb; I give you that. You put two and two together, like they say, and came up with the same answer—the girl you was hired to find is a pervert and a murderer."

I lighted a cigarette with all the enthusiasm of a drowning man taking a drink of water. Les cleared his throat delicately and scraped a nostril with a thumbnail. The room began to smell of pipe tobacco.

"Reckon I'll have to find her myself," Blauvelt observed. "Can't have her going around killing any more women. Tell me how much you got on where she is."

I shrugged. "I'm as far away as the day I started. Farther, in fact."

"Uh-hunh." He nodded heavily. "Them that could've told you, she killed."

"They were killed," I said. "I don't know who killed them."

His face took on lines of reproach. "Well now, it must've been Fremont. It don't figure any other way. You ain't going to try and cover up on her, are you? A dame like that?"

"I don't cover killers, Captain. Didn't I tell you that? Not when I know they're killers."

"Are we supposed to wait around until you make up your mind if she's the one?"

I didn't say anything, just kept on looking at him and not flinching. His sleepy eyes turned even sleepier.

"Look, Pine, you don't want to try and be tough, do you? I don't advise it."

"I'm not tough," I said hotly. "I wouldn't know how. I'm doing my job the only way I know how to do it. I have no solid idea where Laura Fremont is. All I can do is make guesses and test them out. It's not the best way but it's my way and it's not copyrighted."

"And you got nothing to tell me?"

"No."

"No other women you know of that might lead you to the Fremont dame?"

"No."

He leaned forward and shoved out a forefinger at me the size of a salami. "Let me ask you something—what the lawyers call a hypothetical question. Let's say you was to find somebody who knew where Fremont was hiding out. Let's say this somebody told you she was going to turn the information over to the cops instead of giving it to you. How would you feel about it?"

"Oh, hell," I said in disgust. "Why the long way around? Put it out where we both can see it and get it over with."

"That's not an answer," he said with the true dignity only a big-bodied man can put across. "You got a way of handling things and I got a way. This is mine."

"All right," I said, trying to stay calm. "I'd tell her to go to the nearest police station and speak her piece. What did you expect, that I'd try to buy her off?"

He sank back and put his pipe in his mouth. In that mouth it looked like a junior-grade toothpick. His sigh was like something out of last night's windstorm. Everything about him said the first act was over, the audience had put out its cigarettes and got rid of the empty pop bottles and was back in the seats for act two. Les pried himself off the door molding and came over to lean on the back of Blauvelt's chair and watch me out of X-ray eyes.

"The gun you was packing yesterday," the captain said mildly. "A .38 as I remember. Colt, wasn't she? You won't mind if I was to look it over again?"

I gave him the fishy eye. "Somebody been shot, Captain?"

"In this town—" he sighed—"somebody's always getting shot. You wouldn't believe how many a day. Guy's wife burns the toast—bang! Dice don't hit the alley wall twice in a row—bang! How about the gun, Pine?"

"I could tell you it was in the repair shop," I said. "Or I lent it to a friend who left for Burbank, California, this morning."

"Or it fell down a sewer." He puffed smoke from the corner of his mouth. "I wouldn't believe that one either. I got no paper to say you have to. That was a mistake, I guess."

I got up and went into the bedroom, took the gun out of its underarm holster and brought it into the living room. I put it down on the coffee table between us and sat down again and said nothing.

Blauvelt made a vague gesture and Les was over to the gun like a cocker spaniel after a stick. He had it apart quicker than I could have set the safety catch. It was a pleasure to watch him. He smelled the muzzle and the breach and his ears seemed to quiver. He went to the nearest window and held the gun up to the light and squinted into the barrel—and managed not to lick his chops. He said nothing. He didn't have to. He came back to the table and put the gun together with no waste motions, set the safety and laid the works in one of Blauvelt's square paws.

"Clean," Les said. "Too clean. Done very recently, maybe inside an hour or two. No dust and it stinks of fresh oil. Uses Remington .38 Short Colt cartridges; lead."

Blauvelt didn't say anything. I didn't say anything. Les went around behind the chair again and rested on his laurels.

I moved my toes inside my shoes and waited. There was some silence. Finally Captain Blauvelt leaned the gun barrel against one of his knees.

"Rogers Park got a call this morning," he said, watching my necktie. "Some janitor sees a woman sitting in a Buick sedan about six o'clock. Hour or so later she's still there; same position and everything. He goes over to see if she's sleeping maybe. She's asleep, all right—a bullet in her head and no gun in sight——"

"I see," I said, interrupting him. "No gun, so you thought of mine. That follows."

"She was identified," he said, not hearing me. "A Mrs. Bonnie Field O'Flynn, night-club owner. Or her husband owns it, that is. Guess which night club."

"Why stop now?" I sneered.

"Yeah. We got it at Sheffield on the teletype. I arranged for Les to go out and see O'Flynn. He gave us quite a bit of information, Pine. Seems his wife had a private talk with a private dick last evening at the club—after the private dick talked to him first. He's kind of sore at you, brother. And he's plenty tough."

"He's a handful of nothing," I said. "He bluffs easy. A hangnail would put him to bed for a week."

He shook his head, almost sadly. "He thinks you shot his wife. Says he'll swear you threatened to kill her because she was going to turn certain information over to the police. You're in a spot, pal."

"This a pinch, Captain?"

"They got the bullet out," he went on, talking to himself and smiling faintly over how nice everything was fitting today. "Slug from a .38. Lead—and no steel jacket or nothing like that. From a short gun, seems like, else it would've gone all the way through and then some. Ballistics is doing a blow-up on it. Ought to have some nice pictures along about now. Then again it might take another twenty-four hours. The lab at Central is short of men, I hear. And they'll want something for comparison purposes."

He lifted the gun, hefted it, tapped a forefinger on the barrel. "Think I'll kind of take this along," he said mildly. "If you don't mind, naturally. Les could write you out a receipt for it. He writes a real clear hand."

"You and your hypothetical questions," I said.

The gun slid into one of his side pockets while he bent over to knock his pipe ashes into the tray. He stood up, taking his hat off the floor on the way, and ran a hand absently along the rough material of the chair's back.

"I don't think a bullet out of your gun will match the one they took out of her," he said, "or you'd of got rid of it and said you lost it or it was swiped and that way made me work hard. Or maybe you thought I'd think that. Which would make you even smarter than I figured. Anyway, stick around where I can find you if the time comes to find you. Hear me?"

Les opened the door for him, not quite with a flourish. Blauvelt turned his shoulders enough to get them through without scraping any varnish off the frame and walked along the hall to the elevator, the sergeant two steps behind him.

They were quite a combination. I didn't laugh at them.

I went back in and closed the door with a kind of tenderness, as if I wouldn't have the opportunity of closing it many more times, and went over to sit on the couch and finish my cigarette over some thoughts.

The sand was running out. My time was almost up. The minute Blauvelt learned a test bullet from my gun matched the lump of lead removed from Bonnie O'Flynn's head he'd be out after me and the cell door would yawn wide.

Nobody left now but the rich Mrs. Lawrence Griswold. Eve Shelby Griswold. Throw a bluff at her. Throw it hard enough to loosen a few teeth. There were some facts to throw to give the bluff body. Facts like her good friend Stu Whitney being in this thing up to his neck. You used to work at the Tropicabana, Mrs. Griswold. So did three other dames, all of them tied in at one time or another with Laura Fremont and Grace Rehak—and all of them now dead because of it. Why, you even used to room with one of them, Mrs. Griswold! A cute little Lesbian named Mary Conrad, remember? Thing is, were you rooming with her under the name of Laura Fremont or Grace Rehak? Either way, you'd have something to hide, and that something you're hiding is why you might have killed her and the other two. Got a nice iron-bound alibi for one-thirty this morning, Mrs. Griswold? You'd better have. Ever been around a certain LaSalle Street rooming house? There's a gray-haired rail of a landlady out there I'd like you to meet. Uses the word *whom* like a sword—a sword with two edges.

No doubt about it: Eve Griswold was definitely the one to

see. But no phone call first. No percentage in warning her, putting her on guard. Besides, Stu Whitney or Ruth Abbott had probably told her all about me by this time. Way to do it was just breeze out there, talk fast and listen to nobody, and bust right into her boudoir. It wasn't as if we hadn't been formally introduced.

It was getting along toward one o'clock according to my strap watch. Lake Ridge was a healthy drive up along the North Shore. Clear into Lake County—millionaire's row. Got to look right to make the grade up there.

I blew the lint off my hat and went out to find a barber shop.

CHAPTER 21

It was about what I expected. Huge estates behind stone walls and ornamental iron and towering hedges, all put up to insure that special brand of privacy which the idle rich appear to value above everything else. In the tall trees birds made the kind of sounds birds make everywhere, but not quite so loud, as if afraid they might annoy some aged moneybags at his midday nap. The district wasn't laid out in nice even squares the way city blocks are. Out here the boundary lines depended on how much ground you owned, and many of the plots were acres in size.

Avon Road was a curving length of crushed rock that glistened whitely under the warm sun. Lake Michigan muttered and rolled somewhere close by but out of sight. I passed two cars in as many miles along the road—one a long low station wagon as rakish as a pirate ship, the other a dark-blue town car with a uniformed chauffeur up front and, in back, a matron on her way into town to pick up a mink-lined garbage pail.

The entrance to 1124 was a double wrought-iron gate between fieldstone pillars set in a fifteen-foot hedge of blue-green white pine. Sunlight against the hedge glinted on metal here and there, indicating it was backed up with a stout steel fence. Beyond the gates a wide gleaming concrete driveway curved from view behind another hedge that was not so tall as the first but still tall enough to hide everything beyond it.

There was a strip of gravel between the road and the outer hedge. I swung the Plymouth onto the strip twenty feet below the driveway and got out. There was no sidewalk. Sidewalks were for people who walked once in a while outdoors. I stood there in the drowsy air with the smell of flowers and distant water coming to me and brushed tobacco ash out of my lap and made sure the crease in my hat was what *Esquire* would quote in the next issue. I smoothed my hair with my hand, put the hat back on and walked over to the driveway and up it to the gate.

No one in sight. A bird sang in one of a row of massive elms beyond the inner hedge. That and the whisper of a breeze among branches and the faraway whir of an electric lawn mower were the only sounds. I looked at a massive milk-white globe on top of each of the two pillars, at the black spears that made up the gates and at the locked bolt that might have come out of some medieval castle only wasn't as easy to get by. I was thinking of opening my mouth and sounding off with a rebel yell when I caught sight of a white push button set in the side of one pillar.

I pushed it. Nothing happened, I heard nothing, no geni oozed out of either frosted globe. Then feet came at a moderate pace along concrete and an elderly man with a seamed outdoor face came around the left post and looked at me through the ironwork.

"This the Griswold estate?" I asked.

"Yep. What'll it be?"

"Open up," I said. "I'm late now."

He didn't stir. "Sellin' somethin', mister?"

"You ask everybody who comes along that question?"

"Nope. Just them that look like they'd be sellin' somethin'."

So much for my best suit and the handkerchief in my breast pocket. I said, "I'm here to see Mrs. Griswold."

"What's the name?"

I told him the name. He didn't leap to unlock the gate.

"She expectin' you?"

"Not at any special time. Tell her it's the man about the roulette wheel."

He left me and clumped over to the nearest pillar and took a stand-up phone from a niche there. He gave my name and what I had said to whoever was at the other end. After a while he put the phone back, took a key from his pocket and unlocked a section of grillwork forming a door in the gate itself.

"Follow the driveway," he told me. He locked up after me and wandered off the way he had come, toward a redwood cottage behind a bank of bushes and climbing vines twenty feet down the hedge.

I tramped along the curving ribbon of concrete, past velvety lawns and molded dark-green hedges and still more lawns, past trees and bushes and flower beds and rose gardens. My legs began to complain at all the exercise they were getting.

Finally the driveway skirted a shoulder of hedge and I was looking across enough lawn to hold a steeplechase, with the main house beyond that. Architects probably came for miles to see it. Three floors of somebody's idea of early Norman, with leaded glass and casements and heavy protruding beams, and looking as though it had been old at the time everybody was sore about the Louisiana Purchase. It looked bigger than most state hospitals and about as inviting.

I went up under a porte-cochere and rang the bell and hoped for the best. The door retreated silently and a man in livery, tall and spare with the face of an Indian chief, ushered me into a circular hall that went up two stories to a stained-glass skylight. The tapestries hanging on the walls would either be Gobelin or thrown out. Three suits of armor, complete with early armet helmets and halberds, stood around, looking the size of chessmen in all that immensity.

The man took my hat and got rid of it. "Mr. Pine? Madame is waiting."

We went through a vaulted opening and along a wide corridor to an elevator standing open and waiting. We rode up to the top floor and I was led along another corridor and around a bend and still another corridor with one wall solid glass overlooking the lake rolling with a ground swell. It looked bright and deadly under the early afternoon sun. Almost at the end of this my guide stopped and opened a door, and I went past him and in.

It was a bright and happy room, big but not actually appearing to be big. One wall was shelves holding record albums, hundreds upon hundreds of them, all indexed and alphabetized. A custom-built phonograph in a carved rosewood cabinet stood in a recess across the room, a solid row of windows beyond it. There was a concert grand piano with a bust of Mozart on a wide scarf, and busts of other fast boys with a piano were scattered tastefully about the place. There was a large fireplace across from the records. The usual assortment of tables, chairs, couchs and desks—all rosewood and fragile—were placed about the room. This was the music room—probably one of twelve in a place this size.

She was sitting on a window seat near the phonograph, one leg drawn under her, wearing an afternoon frock in figured white. Her blonde hair had a plain gold barrette holding it off her face. She wore very little make-up and a single, very short strand of pearls at her neck—wedding and engagement rings were on the correct hand. A smart woman would want to be photographed looking exactly that way. And then I remembered that Eve Griswold didn't like being photographed.

If she was frightened or worried it didn't show. Her smile was cordial but reserved. I thought her eyes looked a little tired. Perhaps she had been up all night clipping bond coupons.

"I know you," she said, after we had looked at each other for a long moment. "I'm sorry but I'd forgotten your name. You're the man who plunged at roulette last night."

"How do you do, Mrs. Griswold. I'm the one."

She laughed. Musically, not long and not loudly. "I couldn't imagine. Granger said it was about a roulette wheel. We don't have one, although my husband has put enough on them to own hundreds."

I smiled politely and looked slowly around the room. She said, "Do sit down. Here, next to me."

I sat on the other end of the window seat. She eyed me with frank interest. "What happened to your eye? If you don't mind my asking."

"A man hit it. Do you mind if I smoke?"

"Of course not. May I have one, too?"

We blew smoke, on a friendly basis. Outside I could see a sliver of the lake beyond a clump of sprawling oaks and four tennis courts behind wire. Off to one side was an oblong swimming pool, country-club size, and a cluster of red-roofed dressing rooms.

I said, "I'm a private detective, Mrs. Griswold. I hope you don't mind entertaining me in that capacity."

"Heavens, no! Why should I?" Her blue eyes got very round but she was laughing behind them. "You're not going to serve me with papers, or whatever men in your line do, are you?"

"No. Just that I need a little light thrown on a matter and I think maybe you can throw it."

"Well! This *is* exciting. I'll do what I can."

"I understand you worked at the Tropicabana prior to your marriage," I said. "I'm checking on a couple of girls employed there at the time."

"Who are they? Of course, Steve O'Flynn could probably tell you much more than I can."

"Not what I want to know, he can't. Mary Conrad is one."

Her eyes narrowed a little. "Mary? Why, she's still out there. One of the chorus."

"You know her well?"

"Oh, I guess so. As well as show girls ever get to know one another."

"I heard it a little different," I said. "You roomed with her at one time, didn't you?"

The question didn't seem to bother her. "Well, yes. But only briefly and a long time back."

"Would that be on Surf Street?"

"It might have been," she said carelessly. "Around that part of town anyway. That was the time I did a lot of moving around. Four or five places in as many months. Why not ask Mary? She might recall."

She was either one hell of an actress or she was neither of the two girls I was trying to find, and Stuart Whitney had told her nothing. "Mary is past recalling," I said. "She's dead. Murdered."

Her eyes turned blank with horror and surprise. "How . . . awful! I can hardly believe it When did it happen?"

"Yesterday," I said, feeling I was telling her something she had known all along. "Around three in the afternoon."

"And I saw her only a few nights ago." She shivered a little. "Did they get the man who did it?"

I stared steadily into her eyes. "Did a man kill her, Mrs. Griswold?"

Some of the friendliness faded from her face. "I don't

know, naturally. This is the first I've heard of it. What did happen?"

"She was strangled with a stocking. In her own apartment. A woman did the job."

"And why have you come to tell me about it?"

"You were one of her best friends. I'm surprised you weren't notified by somebody from the club. I had an idea you might know of some woman who had a reason to do her in."

She drew deeply on her cigarette. Her expression was growing a trifle strained. "Certainly not. I doubt if Mary had an enemy in the world."

"She must have had some funny friends," I said. "You should have seen her."

She shuddered openly. "I'm glad I didn't. Would you care for a drink? I think I need one."

"Thanks. Anything at all."

She leaned forward to press a button behind the phonograph. "I'm sorry if I seem a little heartless about this. I'm not, really. But Mary and I have had nothing in common for a long time."

"She was a Lesbian, I understand," I said, making it sound very casual.

She lifted one of her solid eyebrows at me. "She may have been. I hope you don't think I have any of that about me."

"It would be a horrible waste if you were."

She almost grinned. The door opened and a brown-haired slip of a girl in a maid's uniform came in. "Yes, madame?"

"Highballs, Irene. Scotch will do, I think. You may as well bring in a cart."

"Yes, madame." She went out the door, closing it like the baby was asleep.

I flicked ash in the ash stand drawn up in front of us and

said, "About Mary Conrad. She had a friend named Purcell —Ellen Purcell. That jog anything in you?"

"Purcell?" she repeated. "It sounds vaguely fam——" Her head went back sharply. "Why, that's the girl who was —who was——"

"—also murdered," I said, finishing it for her. "Yeah. This begin to take on a meaning to you now?"

"Exactly what meaning is it supposed to take on?" Her voice was rising slightly.

"Ellen was another member of the old crowd, Mrs. Griswold. Ellen Purcell, Mary Conrad, Bonnie Field, Grace Rehak, Laura Fremont. You remember Grace, don't you?"

The door opened again and Irene came in, wheeling what might have been an oversize tea cart, but was actually a miniature bar. I watched her put together two tall drinks, using pinch-bottle Scotch and charged water, with ice cubes from a freezing unit inside. She put one glass in Eve Griswold's hand and the other in mine. It had a cool, friendly feel, like a lake breeze on a sultry night.

When the door closed I drank some of my drink and waited for Eve Griswold to do the same. She lowered her glass and stared at me round-eyed. "Where were we?"

"Talking about Grace Rehak."

"Who is Grace Rehak?"

"A former hooker. She may be almost anything today."

"What's a hooker?"

"I thought you used to work in a night-club?"

"Oh, you mean a prostitute?"

"Yeah. That was Gracie. A two-buck broad."

Her shrug indicated distaste for the subject. "I can't say I think much of your kind of job."

"I never had a chance to marry money," I said.

Anger darkened her cheeks. It made her look even better.

"Perhaps you'd better leave," she said haughtily. "I don't like remarks like that."

"Then don't call for them. I chose my type of work of my own free will."

She glowered at me, then leaned into her drink like Ted Williams leaning into a fast ball. Her throat muscles rippled smoothly and her firm breasts pushed against the figured material of her dress. When she lowered the glass it was empty of everything except ice cubes.

She reached for one of the bottles. "It may interest you to know I love my husband, Mr. Pine. Let me make you another drink."

"Love is why women marry at all, isn't it?" I said. "Not too much Scotch; it's a little early in the day for serious guzzling."

She put in enough to float an anvil, giving herself the same treatment. What with the ice, there was hardly enough room for soda. She leaned sideways and handed me the glass, her arm brushing mine. Her nails were long, pointed and very red.

We drank. The warmth of the liquor crawled up from my belly and tried to lift my head like a balloon.

"I'd like another cigarette," she said huskily.

I gave her one and held a match. Our hands touched. My skin tingled. She smiled slowly and her eyes were almost luminous.

"You were telling me how much you love your husband," I said. "How does he feel about it?"

"There's no other woman for him. He trusts me completely and God help anybody that tries to hurt me."

"Why tell me?"

Her eyes wavered. "Why not? We're just talking."

We drank. Deeply. I said, "Tell me about Stuart Whitney, Mrs. Griswold."

She looked down into her glass and hesitated just long enough for me to realize she was hesitating. When she looked up again her expression was open and a little puzzled.

"Stu? What about him? I thought you knew Stu."

"Only to nod to. How long have you known him?"

"Why . . . I don't know exactly. It's been months and months."

"How long has he lived at the Barryshire?"

She moved a shoulder. "Three months—maybe four."

"Where did he live before that?"

She laughed shortly. "Why all this interest in Stu Whitney? Has *he* been up to something?"

"It's too early to tell. Where did he live when you first met him?"

"Some small residential hotel on Winthrop, near Devon," she said. "I'm afraid that's the best I can do. Why not take this up with him?"

"I know those hotels," I said. "Sixty-five a month buys the best they've got to offer."

We finished our drinks and this time *I* made new ones. I gave her time to test the mixture, then said, "Let's talk about him some more. Whitney, I mean. How did you happen to meet him?"

She looked at me sideways, a thoughtful line in the clear skin above her eyes. "Nothing unusual about it. I was singing in a small night club out on Belmont Avenue. Stu used to drop in and one night we got to talking over a drink or two. Right after that he introduced me to some of the girls working at the Tropicabana. That led to an introduction to Steve O'Flynn and Steve put me on."

We drank again. The liquor was beginning to let me know

that Scotch was thicker than water. I shook my head slightly to clear it and took up the chase. "You still see quite a bit of him?"

One of her eyebrows arched. "Why not? Stu's a lot of fun. He squires me around now and then when Larry gets tied up."

"How does your husband feel about it?"

Her lips flattened with annoyance. "Oh, come off it, Pine! Larry knows Stu Whitney means nothing to me other than as an occasional escort."

I said, "I don't get it. I really don't. Any guy who's working at his fourth marriage should know something about women. Yet he lets you gallop around with some slick-haired playboy who likes a well-turned curve as well as the next and never quivers a whisker. No wonder he can't hang on to a woman."

She polished off what was left in her glass and grabbed the bottle again. What she took almost emptied it but there was another full one three inches away.

"You're missing the point," she said. She slurred the second word a fraction; the stuff was beginning to take a toehold on her. "Larry's first wife was all right, from what I hear. She died six, seven years ago and it tore hell out of him. He tried to cure the pain by getting another wife fast. She was a gold-digging little bitch and shook him down quick and got out with half a million bucks as a settlement. Six months later he reached in the grab bag again and did even worse. That one faded even faster and Larry's bankroll got another dent in it. Then he went overboard for me.

"But here's where the story gets different, Pine. I went all out for him. If he hadn't had a dime I'd have felt the same way. Nobody believes it—nobody! I get the quirked eyebrow from every two-bit bum I pass in the street. They know all the answers, do the so-smart little people. 'Torcher marries millionaire. Love?—don't make me laugh!' They don't have to say it out loud; I can read it in their smug faces."

Half of it was the liquor talking. The flush in her face deepened as I watched. The brittle, high-society air she had thrown at me when I first arrived had gone down for the third time in pinch-bottle Scotch and I was getting pure night-club singer with a burden of bitterness to unload.

"There's more, Pine—one hell of a lot more! When I walked into this art gallery I found it loaded with old family retainers that had spent so much time looking down their noses at Larry's previous two wives there wasn't any way for them to get over it. To them I was just another cat that wanted her claws gold-plated."

She tore into her glass again. The stuff would be coming out of her ears next. I tilted my own glass from force of bad habit and said nothing at all.

"Far as the servants go, it was easy," Eve Griswold said moodily. "I fired the lot of them and got in some people that could call me 'madame' without straining it through their teeth. But then I got handed the tough one—and I've never been able to lick it."

Her lovely face turned a little sad, a little hard. She shifted her position on the window seat and crossed her knees carelessly. I saw a long length of the best in legs in the best of nylon.

She said, "There's a stepdaughter. She'd love to spread my guts on a windy hill. I don't say I blame her, after the kind of specimens Larry usually dragged up to his bed. I did my damnedest to show her I was in this because I thought as much of her old man as she did—every bit as much! You think she'd even give me a chance to prove it? Not a nickel's worth. I swear to Christ, Pine, there's something wrong with that girl. She thinks every woman Larry gives a kind word to is going to be her new stepmother the following week. I got a bellyful of her quick. Now she keeps away from me and I keep away from her. Thank God the place is big enough!"

She stopped to drink again. I felt vaguely uncomfortable, as if I was watching a cripple take a bath. I said, "Well, you never know. Seeing your party at the Tropicabana last night I had an idea Lawrence Griswold might be getting ready for a new Mrs. Griswold. Like that redhead with the notebook, for instance."

"Ruth?" She stared at me emptily. "Hell, she's a vegetable! I figured I could use a social secretary and Stu Whitney dug her up for me somewhere. She knows her business but that's all I can say for her."

"That's interesting," I said. "Her and Whitney, huh?"

She made a derisive sound that was half hiccough. "Are you serious? Ruth Abbott? She wouldn't sit in the same room with a man unless somebody else was around. Larry accidentally brushed a hand against her hip one day in the library. I thought she was going to climb the wall."

She swung up her glass and emptied it down her throat. I expected her to fall off the seat after that one. Instead she reached for the bottle. She knocked over two glasses and the ice tongs, but she got it. She poured in plenty, forgetting to add water. A strand of her golden-blonde hair slipped its moorings and dropped down over one eye. She shoved it back, dislodging more hair in the process. She looked like an angel—a drunken angel whose halo had slipped.

Eve Griswold put her head back against one of the window frames and stared silently at me. I finished what was in my glass, put it down and leaned back next to one of her flawless shoulders. Our faces were inches apart. Her thin nostrils flared ever so slightly and the bodice of her dress stirred under uneven breathing. Her eyes seemed to mist over, to deepen almost to blackness.

"Why did you come here?" she said abruptly. "What are you after?"

"You already know," I said thickly. "You knew before I came in that door. And you've been shivering inside ever since. Even a gallon of the best Scotch hasn't been able to warm you."

"You're crazy," she said through stiffened lips. "You goddam snoop, you're crazy. Go away."

I kept on looking into her eyes. She twisted her head away and drank. Straight whisky—enough to curl armor plate. She shuddered violently and almost dropped the glass. I took it from her and set it next to mine on the bar top. I turned and took hold of her shoulders and brought my face close to hers. Her breath was warm and moist, as breath should be; her lips were ever so slightly parted and waiting; the odor of clean cared-for skin came up from under the neckline of her dress.

I put my mouth hard against hers. For a moment it was like kissing a warmed-over corpse. And then the lips came to life under mine and soft arms lifted and slid around my neck. Her body strained up hard against me, the heat of her firm unbound breasts filtered through my shirt . . . and this was no longer an experiment.

She drew away with a sudden hard movement and looked at me out of drugged eyes. "Damn you," she muttered. "What are you trying to prove? That you're irresistible—or that I can be had?"

"Maybe both," I said. "Maybe neither. Maybe because under the right conditions a man acts like a man. The hell with it. You're a woman in love with your husband. Or did you forget?"

"Not even for a second," she said with deadly calm. "No matter what I do, I keep what I value."

"Uh-hunh. And damn the cost. If it means paying blackmail, you'll pay it. If it means knocking off a few dames, off they go. No price too high; no method too low."

She had turned to stone. I lighted a cigarette and got off the window seat to stretch my legs. I stood there and looked down at her and felt the muscles of my face begin to ache from the twisting of my lips.

"The whole stinking picture is unrolling," I said. "You're through, baby. Only one dark corner left and we'll let the boys in blue throw the light on that.

"Your real name is what I'm talking about. Not that it really matters; they can fry you just as crisp under any name. You're either Gracie Rehak, the former can-house cutie; or you're Laura Fremont, killer of Ellen Purcell. But for my money you're still Lizzie Borden."

I poured some liquor in my glass and drank it down and put the glass back on the bar. "The cops will get what's lacking, Mrs. Griswold. They'll shake the facts out of Stuart Whitney, the guy who stumbled onto your little secret and made the most of it. They can always check your bank account for withdrawals and his bank account for deposits. If they jibe pretty well on dates and amounts, that will help. There'll be other ways, and by the time the law has what they need, Whitney will sing it in three sharps. You should have let him have a bullet or two while you were at it."

All she did was look at me. I knew I would see those eyes as they were then in my sleep for months afterward.

I turned and left the room.

CHAPTER 22

I WAS almost to the bend in the corridor when one of the doors along it opened a crack and a tanned hand beckoned. The party behind the door and the hand was Susan Griswold. She was slim and smart in brown silk shantung and open-toed brown pumps. She looked cool and intense about something.

She took hold of my sleeve and pulled me through and shut the door softly. Her blue-gray eyes flashed. "I saw you come in. What did you think of her?"

"She'd make a wearing week end," I said. "But it would probably be worth it."

She colored. "That's a nice uninhibited way of looking at it, I suppose. What did you find out?"

"Everything. Everything, that is, that she wanted me to find out. Plus the fact that she could drink me under the bench any Friday in the week."

A small cold smile touched her lips. "I told you she was clever. Now you can see how hard it will be for me to get her out of here before she does any real damage."

I looked past her at the room. A bedroom—but only for those born to the purple. Anybody else would hang their clothes out the window and sleep in one corner of its rug.

She jabbed me in the chest with a short blunt-nailed forefinger. "What's the next step? You're not going to quit, are you? I thought you strong silent detectives were half bulldog and half bloodhound."

"I did what I could, Miss Griswold. I threw my best bluff in her teeth and stalked out. It was a good strong bluff, a lot of meat on it in the shape of some facts not to be explained away as coincidences, and it may jolt her into doing the wrong thing. Not that she has to—and not that she will if she holds still long enough to count up to ten. There's too little actual proof against her and far too much money behind her for the cops to make an attempt to pin even one murder rap on her. Everything's in her favor, including the fact that none of the three corpses is headline material."

She gaped at me, the freckles showing again. "Three? What three? Are you saying she killed three different people?"

"She could have. That's as far as I can take it. All we can do—all *I* can do—is hope for her to crack up in time to save me from rotting in jail while waiting for my trial to come up."

Nothing could be blanker than her expression. "Why you? You're not involved; you told me so on the phone early last night."

"Uh-hunh. I forgot to touch wood when I said it. I think I'll be running along. Nice place you have here, Miss Griswold. The memory of it during the long nights behind bars will cheer me up."

Her lip curled. "So you're quitting. Down comes the flag and you hand over your sword with a small bow and a wisecrack. You certainly fooled me, little man."

I sighed. "Mind your tongue. I'm not quitting, although I'd like to. The time has come for me to sit down with a bottle and a hypodermic and think. Mixed in somewhere with all the information I've picked up in the past twenty-four hours is the key to this puzzle. I'm going someplace and mull. I've always been good at mulling; this time I'll have to be perfect."

I tipped a hand at her and walked out. The elevator was waiting. I rode down to the first floor and looked around for the guy who had my hat. I didn't see him but I saw something else. I saw two people standing in the open double doorway to what looked like the north wing of the public library. They stood there, not talking, not moving, frozen like flies in amber.

They were Stuart Whitney and Ruth Abbott.

Sudden anger turned over in me. I walked over to them. "The vultures gather," I said. "She's upstairs, Whitney, getting out the checkbook and shaking the pen. But get enough this time for a get-away stake. Blackmail is still a felony in this state."

Neither of them said anything. They waited with faces filled with hate, waited for me to pick up and go. I looked at their hatred, enjoying it, wishing there was even more of it for me to enjoy.

I tried again. "It's only right to tell you, she may be a little difficult today. I happened to let slip how nice a black net nightgown and red hair can fit in with that color scheme at the Barryshire."

All it did was make Ruth Abbott breathe through her mouth. I could see a tiny smear of lipstick on one of her teeth, like a ferret that had been at the chickens.

This was childish. No other word for it. Formless anger can do that to the best of us. And I was not the best; I had never realized it as clearly as I was realizing it now.

I hitched up my diaper and left them. I went on and on until I came out into the huge circular hall. The man in livery was coming down a different corridor toward me. I reached out and patted the shoulder of one of the suits of armor. "Done any Holy Grailing lately?" I said aloud.

And that was childish too.

The man with the Indian face located my hat and handed it to me. He said "Good afternoon, sir," very politely and opened the door. The sun shone and the green lawns beckoned and the air was exactly the right density and odor for breathing.

And between me and all that were three men coming up under the porte-cochere. Lawrence Griswold, followed by Captain Blauvelt and the sergeant.

CHAPTER 23

No GUNS jumped out to cover me. Lawrence Griswold gave me a long level stare that had no warmth in it and said, "I met these officers at the gate. They insisted you were here. I want to know why you are here."

I said, "No use standing here with the door open. We're letting in the flies."

Nobody moved. There weren't any flies anyway. Griswold's jaw set. "You're a private detective named Pine. What business do you have forcing your way into my home?"

I shook my head. "If I'm going to answer any questions it'll be while I'm sitting down. And not on the front stoop either."

Blauvelt's square heavy face was without expression, his yellow eyes half closed. "We'll take him along, Mr. Griswold," he rumbled. "Whatever reason he was here we'll get it out of him and let you know."

If Lawrence Griswold heard him he gave no sign of it. To me, he said, "I want one answer now, please. Who did you come here to see?"

"Your wife, Mr. Griswold."

The hollows under his cheekbones deepened microscopically. "Very well, Mr. Pine. I'll talk this over with you in my office." He glanced around at Captain Blauvelt. "I'll try to make it brief, sir. You and your man can wait in the library."

"Well now," Blauvelt began in an injured tone.

But I beat him to it. "No more private talks, Mr. Griswold. You've got a right to be in on this, since it does concern your wife. But I'm through trying to bank my shots into the corner pocket. Any questions will be answered where the captain can listen in."

He wasted no time arguing about it. "As you wish," he said formally and the three of them pushed past me and we were standing in the big circular hall with the door closed.

The captain avoided my eyes. He said, "Les," and the sergeant put his hat between his knees to hold it and used both hands to pat me under the arms and around the waist. He stepped back and moved the hat up under one arm and said, "He's clean, Chief."

The silence got a little heavy before I noticed it. The three of them were looking strangely at me. I didn't blame them. I got my jaw up off my collarbone and said, in a voice I hardly recognized, "Change of plans. There's been a small miracle. This is going to be open house. Get them all into the library, Mr. Griswold."

He swallowed. "I don't believe I——"

"Everybody," I said. "Mrs. Griswold, Stuart Whitney, Susan Griswold and Ruth Abbott."

Griswold tried to keep his temper but it wasn't easy. "I see no reason——"

I interrupted him. "This is going to end up in the State's Attorney's office eventually. It's got to. Maybe we can strain out some of the details beforehand—details that will do no good by being aired. Humor me a little, Mr. Griswold; I've earned it."

Griswold's handsome face had taken on a grayish cast at mention of the State's Attorney. Blauvelt was petting the brim of his hat with the first two fingers of his left hand and making up his mind. He said, "I kinda figured you'd turn out to be one of the smart alecks." He sighed like a blacksmith's bellows. "Guess we'll have to put this off, Mr. Griswold. These things get handled in a routine way and this ain't it. I'm taking Pine in and I'm taking him now."

"I'm not interested in routine or the lack of it," Griswold said acidly. "I want to hear this man's explanation of whatever seems to need explaining. I don't propose to get it secondhand."

The captain put on his dignified expression. "You're talking to an officer of the law," he rumbled. "I can't see you obstructing justice—not a prominent man like you, Mr. Griswold. I'm charging Pine with suspicion of murder and I'm taking him outa here. Right now!"

Indecision seeped into Griswold's expression. I said, "Don't be silly, Blauvelt. Right now you're in no position to hand out even a parking ticket. You're not only out of your district, brother; you're not even in Cook County."

He moved his eyes to look at the sergeant. The sergeant's face was as blank as a hermit's appointment book. The captain's eyes shifted again, this time to one of the suits of armor. And there they stuck.

I said, "Let's try the library, Mr. Griswold."

The chairs and couch were green leather; three of the walls were solid books, the fourth nothing but French windows. There were eight of us, all down at the far end of the room and looking lost in all the immensity. There was liquor and the trimmings on a table in front of one of the room's two fireplaces, cigars in a humidor on a two-acre teakwood table and an undercurrent of emotion made up of many emotions.

Everybody was seated because there was no sense in standing. Some were in chairs and Susan Griswold was on the couch next to Blauvelt. Les was tilted back in a straight chair at one end of what could loosely be called a semicircle, with the other end terminating at the huge desk. In between were Eve Griswold, her husband, Ruth Abbott and Stuart Whitney. In that order and not for any reason, not because anybody had planned it that way. They had straggled in, their faces almost painfully expressionless, and dropped into whatever chair was handy and unfilled.

I leaned my hips and the palms of my hands against the rounded edge of the desk and looked them over, aware of an almost tangible wave of resentment building up against me from nearly everyone in the room.

I said, "A little while ago Mr. Griswold asked me a question. It was a question he had the right to ask and to expect as true an answer as I could give him. In one way or another the answer affects everyone here, which is why we *are* here."

Nobody said anything. Neither had I, actually; I was just warming up the vocal cords.

I said, "A small-town girl came to Chicago a couple of years ago and disappeared a year later. Her name was Laura Fremont and I was hired to find her. Before I left that small town I asked around for a girl who had known Laura Fremont while they both were in high school and who was also in Chicago. Her name was Grace Rehak.

"It didn't take long for me to learn that one of them didn't want to be found. Not only that but other people didn't want her found either. When I got back to Chicago around noon yesterday I hadn't warmed the seat of my office chair before Mr. Whitney, here, breezed in and offered to make me rich if I'd tell him who was interested in Grace Rehak and why."

Every eye in the room slid over to Whitney. He looked as flurried as a ton of coal. He gave me a bored glance and shot one of his spotless cuffs.

"No reason you shouldn't know about that now," he said coolly. "The papers say she was found dead early this morning, so it's no longer a matter of betraying a confidence."

He leaned back to light a cigarette and flip the match into the fireplace. "I knew her as Bonnie Field. We were close friends up until a few months ago when she married Steven O'Flynn. Yesterday she came to me for help. A private detective was hunting her down under her real name—Grace Rehak. It was the first I knew Field wasn't her right name. She hinted her past was nothing to be proud of and she was in absolute terror that her husband would learn the truth from this detective. I agreed to do what I could and she drove me to his office. I offered him money for the right information but he refused." His lip curled. "Evidently I didn't offer him enough."

Whitney stopped there to flick ashes from his cigarette and give me his best sneer. I let it bounce off and float away. "Any more to add to that?" I said politely.

His hard smile said he was now ready to throw the switch. "I'm not sure you'll want it said in front of these two police officers, Pine."

"Spit it out," I growled. "I wear no man's collar."

It was his moment and he made the most of it. "I talked to Bonnie O'Flynn at the Tropicabana last night. She told me she was meeting you on Farwell Avenue, near Sheridan, at one o'clock this morning. The newspapers say her body was found there a few hours later."

It got a stir out of the other guests. They looked at me the way a jury looks at the man they intend sticking in the chair on the first ballot. I could almost see Blauvelt's ears flap.

In the silence I walked over to the table and put a drink together. I looked around at all the vacant faces and said, "Can I fix one for anybody else?"

Nobody accepted, thinking probably that I kept at least one bottle of poison up my sleeve. I went back and pushed myself up on a corner of the desk and crossed my ankles.

I met Lawrence Griswold's troubled eyes and said, "The next installment isn't going to be easy. But it's got to come out. No more secrets, like I said."

He took a deep unsteady breath but his gaze didn't waver. He said, "Please go on." There was nothing unsteady about his voice.

I nodded. "I managed to pick up a lead on a former roommate of Laura Fremont's within an hour of my return from her home town. A girl named Mary Conrad. I went out to see her an hour or two later and found her dead on her bed. But that was only half of it. Blacked out on the living-room floor, Mr. Griswold, was your daughter."

That rocked them all. Griswold came halfway out of his chair and his face was whiter than the handkerchief in his hand. Eve Griswold said, "Why do we sit here and listen to this son of a bitch?"

No one answered that one. The restless eyes had moved to where Susan Griswold sat with a faint, almost absent-minded smile on her lips. I drank from my glass and put it on the desk next to me and lighted a cigarette, suddenly aware of being very tired and nothing I could do about it.

I went on flapping my jaw. "Miss Griswold woke up after a while and we talked things over. She said a woman had socked her and she gave me a torn piece of lace she had managed to rip off the woman before blacking out. By the time we were through talking I knew that Mrs. Griswold had shared a room with Mary Conrad two years before, that she had a nice firm motive for wanting Mary Conrad dead, and that she was getting ready to bump her husband off and take over the family fortune. I also learned that she had picked out the guy she was going to share her money and her widowhood with, but it was some time later before I learned the man was Stuart Whitney."

Lawrence Griswold lunged to his feet. "That's nonsense and you know it! I think this has gone far enough."

There was a general shifting in chairs and a murmur of voices. Eve Griswold hid her face in her hands.

"It might have been nonsense, Mr. Griswold, but I didn't know it," I said. "Particularly since it turns out Laura Fremont roomed with Mary Conrad two years ago—and so did Grace Rehak, although not at the same time. That could mean your present wife is either of those two and not Eve Shelby at all."

Griswold's face was livid. "This—this Rehak woman is dead. You heard that from the man who knew her. What are you getting at, Pine?"

"The truth, I hope," I growled. "Will you for Christ's sake sit down!"

He dropped into his chair, trembling, and the room was as silent as a mausoleum. Into the silence I said:

"I'll tell you why I came out to see your wife today, Griswold. Her background before a year or so ago is as cloudy as my future. Before her marriage she was friendly with three women that I know of. One was Ellen Purcell—and Ellen Purcell was murdered. Another was Mary Conrad—and Mary Conrad was murdered. The third was Bonnie Field—and Bonnie Field was murdered. All three were shoved by a woman. I know that because of the lace torn from the woman who killed Mary Conrad, and because last night Bonnie Field was shot to death with my gun while I was in a car with her. I got a head full of bells out of it myself, but before I blacked out I managed to grab hold of the killer. They were the real thing, Mr. Griswold, no padding there at all.

"There's more. Bonnie Field was not Grace Rehak, although she knew Grace and had agreed to impersonate her long enough to find out what I was up to. When she saw I wasn't buying it last night, she flashed the headlights to signal Grace I wasn't so stupid as I looked and for her to come out from behind whatever she was hiding behind and talk to me herself. What Bonnie overlooked was that her failure to convince me meant she had to die too, since I now must know that she could lead me to Grace Rehak. And die she did."

I stopped and drank and got off the desk to put out my cigarette. Eve Griswold had turned to stone again and a hell of a lot I cared. I walked around in a tight circle and wondered how long a man could wave his tongue before it fell on one of his feet.

"One nail left," I said, "and it's got to be hammered in with the rest of them. Another friend of your wife's, Mr. Griswold, is Stuart Whitney. As soon as Eve Shelby married you, Whitney's own financial position was given a healthy boost. To a dime-store cynic like me that spells blackmail—which can only mean your wife has done something to pay blackmail for."

Griswold glanced once at his wife's stricken face. He got out of his chair like an old man. Nobody could look at him. He went over to the liquor and poured out a small amount and drank it and stood there staring at the glass without seeing it.

"Mr. Pine," he said. His voice croaked. "You have accused my wife of killing three women. You have intimated her real name is Rehak, with a past so foul she must pay blackmail to keep me from learning about it. I tell you now, sir, I believe none of this. I am a wealthy man. Every cent I have, everything I own in the world, will go if need be to clear her of your charges."

It sounded theatrical enough to be phony, as a mixture of grief and sincerity so often does. Eve Griswold put her face in her hands and her shoulders shook under the figured white material. If somebody had shot me dead at the moment, cheers would have rocked the room.

I said, "Before you start calling in defense attorneys and writing checks, let me finish this up."

Something in my voice got through to him. He stared hard at me for a long time, trying to get past my expression. Then he went back to his chair and sank into it and waited.

I leaned against the desk and picked up my glass. "All along," I said, "one angle kept popping up that held the key to this whole stinking mess. I kept pushing it away and that was my mistake. The angle is this: every one of the three dead women was, or had been, a Lesbian."

This time the silence was in hunks thick enough to throw at a passing cat. Susan Griswold stopped in the middle of lighting a cigarette and looked at me thoughtfully. Even Blauvelt's fingers left off tapping his knee.

"Let's assume," I said, "that the killer is a Lesbian, as were the women she killed. Let's take it a step farther and say that the killer is either Grace Rehak or Laura Fremont. That means if we can find out which of the two is a Lesbian, we've got our murderer. All right?"

Nobody said it was all wrong, or even partly wrong. I rubbed a finger along the side of the tall glass in my hand and continued to grind out the words.

"Laura Fremont is a small-town girl, from a decent family and no evil companions. Grace Rehak is from the same small town but there the similarity ends. She came from the wrong side of the tracks and ended up in a joy house run by a Lesbian named Bertha Lund. Of the two, then, it seems a reasonable bet that Grace Rehak is the one to turn queer.

"Both girls come on to Chicago. Laura takes a room at the YWCA and makes a few friends. Let's say that she's still got hay in her hair and wouldn't know a Lesbian if one bit her in the leg. She shares a room with one of them, a girl named Mary Conrad. Mary makes a pass at her and Laura gets sore and moves out. This time she takes an apartment with another girl from the same crowd Mary runs around with, a girl named Ellen Purcell. One night Laura comes home and finds Ellen murdered, a stocking around her throat and scratches on her belly. A murder between Lesbians, with jealousy the motive.

"Laura Fremont is petrified with fear. She's sure the cops will think she did the job and send her to the chair. She doesn't even stop to pack a bag, simply runs out into the night and disappears. She changes her name, her appearance and her whole personality. She stops writing to her folks because she's afraid the cops will catch up with her through them. She gets a job singing in a small night club, goes from it to a bigger and better spot as a singer—and ends up marrying a millionaire."

Lawrence Griswold wasn't an old man any longer. One more minute and he'd have his wallet out and start showering me with green affection. His wife had her eyes on me too, but her expression was too mixed to classify.

"Just to tuck in the last loose end of this section of it," I continued, "let's clear up the blackmail angle. Stuart Whitney knew Laura Fremont. He saw her again after Ellen Purcell was murdered and Laura had taken on her new identity. He recognized her and—when she married money—started bleeding her to keep her secret."

Whitney looked lazily up at me. "You're nuts, Pine, completely nuts. Eve Griswold will tell you as——"

"Save it," I growled. "I want to get this over before my throat gives out." I drank the rest of my drink and rested the glass on my knee and opened fire again.

"Grace Rehak is the killer we're after. When she strangled Ellen Purcell, during a lovers' quarrel, she began to worry that Laura Fremont might be able to clear herself and the cops would hunt for the real killer. So Gracie changed her name and personality and dived for cover. Everything went along fine; the cops scratched around on the case and threw up their hands, as cops will do when the going's tough and no one to prod them. And then the Fremonts hired me to find their daughter."

I left my place at the desk and went over and made another drink, more to be doing something besides talk than because I needed it. I came back, stepping over Stu Whitney's feet, and said:

"Bertha Lund got word to Grace Rehak that I was after her. It scared her into trying to cover her trail. She killed Mary Conrad, then figured maybe cunning would work better than violence. So she talked another old friend into passing herself off on me as the real Gracie in hopes of finding out why I was hunting for her.

"But that backfired, so Bonnie Field had to die to prevent my getting the truth out of her. But by now I had all I needed. I knew who Grace Rehak was and where to find her. It was only a case of laying a hand on her shoulder and pushing her into the arms of the cops. Only she didn't know that I knew—and she doesn't know it even now."

Captain Blauvelt lumbered to his feet, his yellow eyes burning like candles behind glass. "Where is she, Pine?" he said in his purring voice.

"Right here in the room," I said, and bit down hard on my teeth.

Blauvelt's eyes moved from me to Eve Griswold's pale and lovely face, from it to the small cold smile on Susan Griswold's lips, from there to Ruth Abbott. And there they stopped. For a long frozen moment there was no sound in the room—and then Ruth Abbott cried out, "No!" and slumped from the chair in a dead faint.

Blauvelt took one almost sinuous step toward her before I said, "Not her. No."

He turned slowly, confused and not caring for it.

"You passed one woman up," I said. "Grace Rehak is—*Stuart Whitney!*"

The small gun was out of his pocket and coming up before the last word was out of my mouth. I threw my glass at him but it went over his shoulder.

A gun roared. No small gun could make that much noise. Stuart Whitney folded in the middle like an oiled hinge and hit the carpet with his face. The gun fell out of his hand and slid all the way under the couch.

Les was still tilted back in his straight chair. Only now there was a heavy police revolver in his hand, smoke curling up from the muzzle. He blinked up at us. "I been putting in a little extra time on the target range," he said.

CHAPTER 24

Captain Blauvelt rode back to town with me in the Plymouth. For the first mile or so he had little to say, just sat there and puffed on his pipe and looked out at the clean sun on the hedges, trees and an occasional unguarded lawn.

He bent finally and knocked ash into the dashboard tray. "What put you on her, Pine?" He grunted. "I mean on her strong enough to pull the kind of stunt you pulled."

I swung the crate around a curve in the crushed-stone roadway. "How many words do you think I can get through my throat in one day?"

"Go ahead," he said. "Listening don't hurt me none."

"Okay," I said, sighing. "I was in his—her . . . all *right*—in Grace Rehak's apartment last night while she was entertaining Ruth Abbott, her queer girl friend. Grace and I had a few words and when I started to leave I tossed his—Gracie's, damn it!—cigarette lighter into her lap. It went between her legs and hit the floor. That, Captain Blauvelt, sir, was a clue. You know what a clue is, of course."

He hated to say it but there was no other way to find out. "Meaning what?"

"From a book," I said. "*Huckleberry Finn.* Seems Huck put on a woman's dress and tried passing himself off as a girl. He ran into an old woman and she dropped something into his lap and Huck clapped his knees together to catch it.

The old girl pointed out to him that while it's instinctive for a man to do that to hold something, a woman will just as instinctively *spread* her legs and catch it in her skirt. With Stu Whitney it worked exactly the opposite. But it didn't register until Les frisked me this afternoon. He shoved his hat between his knees and held it so, leaving both hands free to do his job. And right there several unrelated pieces of the puzzle began coming together."

Blauvelt settled a little lower on the seat and struck a match. "Might as well let me have them too."

I made the turn south into Sheridan Road before answering him. "Well, like when I was at Whitney's apartment last night, I caught the smell of acetone. Women use the stuff to take polish off their nails. The polish was still on Ruth Abbott's nails, but none on Gracie's, of course, since she was now back to being a man—after shooting Bonnie O'Flynn and conking me on the head less than an hour earlier.

"And another thing: Gracie, as Whitney, came to my office yesterday only a minute or two after I had written Mary Conrad's name on my calendar pad. He—she—must have seen it there and realized Mary could ruin her. Whitney rushed to his apartment, got into a dress and a wig, I suppose, and hurried over to Mary's apartment and strangled her. The scratches on her belly were left there by blunt fingernails. Women's nails are seldom trimmed straight across that way. It all fits in, Captain."

He grunted and said nothing more for several blocks. But he was still chewing things over in his mind, for a little later he said, "The whole cockeyed business of her trying to be a man don't make sense to me. You can't hope to make a thing like that stick for long before you make a bonehead move and give yourself away."

"You're forgetting something," I said. "To all intents and

purposes, Gracie Rehak *was* a man. A lot of masculine women 'cross over' and take on the personality, manner, character and clothing of a man. Except for a few physical differences they *are* men. Hell, you read every so often of some case where a guy has been married for years, held down a job and is highly respected by his neighbors—and then he gets in an accident or something and it turns out he's a woman.

"Same way with Gracie Rehak. She probably was on the edge of crossing over for a long time; then she killed Ellen Purcell and was forced to hide out. What better way than by becoming a man—the one thing she'd wanted to do all along."

When we were back in Chicago, I turned west on Addison Boulevard on the way to the Sheffield station. Not until then did Blauvelt have more to say.

"Worked out all for the best, at that," he rumbled. "Nobody gets hurt except people who don't count anyway. Awhile there I figured I might have to go to bat against I don't know how many millions. I wouldn't of liked that one."

"Four people with their lives snuffed out," I said. "Five counting the kid back in Lincoln, Nebraska. But I feel better now that you've pointed out they don't count."

He looked at me narrowly out of his sleepy yellow eyes. "Don't get noble on me, brother. A bunch of lousy perverts." He leaned out the window to spit and the subject was closed.

While he was getting out in front of the station, I said, "My .38. Do I get it back or don't I?"

He leaned a hand the size of a meat platter on the window ledge and cleared his throat. It sounded like a manhole cover falling off the roof. "You'll get it, mister. I ain't throwing away that ballistics report on it, neither. A guy like you is gonna get into trouble again sometime."

I reached for the gearshift, then let loose of it. "One thing more, Captain. How did you know where to find me this afternoon?"

The edges of his ears reddened. "Well now, I guess we'll have to charge that one up to Les. He's been putting in some of his extra time practicing tail jobs, y'see, and when we left your place around noon, he wanted to stick around and make sure you didn't take a powder."

I grinned, and after a moment he grinned with me. I said, "Another six months and you'll be working for him, Captain."

He was still standing there lighting his pipe when I turned the corner.

CHAPTER 25

WHEN I got down to the office the next morning about eleven, the elevator man gave me a package he had signed for. I pushed up the window to let in some of the bright morning air and let out the smell of yesterday's cigarettes and sat down to open the parcel.

My gun. The boys at the laboratory had failed to clean it after firing a test bullet, but then Blauvelt had mentioned they were shorthanded down there. I spun the cylinder and pointed it at the girl on the Varga calendar and said, "Bing, you're dead," and dropped it into the middle drawer.

It took better than half an hour and three tries to get the letter written. I folded it over and was reaching for a blank envelope when the inner office door opened and Mrs. Lawrence Griswold was standing there.

She had never looked lovelier. She was wearing tobacco brown under a loose tweed coat that reached to her knees. The collar of a white blouse lay neat and trim at her neck and her blonde hair brought along its own light.

"Have a chair," I said, not getting up. "You're looking well this morning."

She sat down in the customer's chair alongside the desk and put a rather large brown leather bag on the corner. She was neither frowning nor smiling and her dark-blue eyes were as deep as the Pacific two hundred miles off the coast of Japan.

"Thank you," she said. "I slept well." She let her eyes stray around the ten by twelve room. "So this is what a private detective's office is like."

"Uh-hunh. Not that it always looks this good. Today is the day they changed the sawdust on the floor."

She didn't smile. I hadn't expected her to. She opened her bag and took out a square French enamel case and a cigarette out of that. I held a match for her and she dropped the case back into the bag and left the bag open.

We sat there and looked at each other for a long time without speaking. Finally she took a deep breath and let it out slowly.

"I want to know why," she said simply.

"I thought you would," I said. I picked up the letter I had just finished writing and shook out the folds and held it out to her, my elbow resting on the desk.

She took a long time reading it, although there weren't more than a dozen lines. She folded it back in the original creases and slid it back across the blotter.

"Then you knew all along I was Grace Rehak," she said slowly.

"You had to be," I said. "Just as Stuart Whitney had to be Laura Fremont. Everything pointed that way. There were any number of things in her background to show she was a Lesbian—a Lesbian who was consciously preparing to switch over to the male side of the ledger. Her mother gave me some of those leads without knowing it. Laura's destroying all pictures of herself before leaving home was one, her taking on a phony name when moving in with Ellen Purcell was still another. She might have gone on thinking about doing it but not taking the step if she hadn't killed Ellen during a paranoiac rage. Fear of the law pushed her over the line."

She rubbed some of the ash from her cigarette into the tray and looked past me out the window at the warm sunlight shimmering there. Her eyes were quiet and thoughtful and a little sad.

"I'd like you to know one thing," she said. "I had no idea Stuart Whitney was Laura Fremont—or even that he was a woman. A few months before I married Larry, Stuart and I met at a bar in the casual way people do. There was something vaguely familiar about him but nothing to make me think of a girl I had only known slightly a long time ago. It wasn't until I was married that he hinted of knowing what I had been . . . back in Lincoln."

She stopped to smooth a fold in her dress and think her thoughts. From far off a siren's scream rose, held and faded, letting in the sound of city streets again like distant surf on a rocky shore.

"I gave him money from time to time," Eve Griswold said. "No talk of blackmail. Just loans that would never be repaid. Then Bertha Lund got word to me about you. I had kept in touch with her because of my father."

It was a full minute before she spoke again. "Anyway, I told Stuart about it—there was no one else I could turn to—and he said not to worry, that he'd take care of it."

She crushed out her cigarette and reached into the bag for the case. I held another match for her, watching the flame burn down and die close to my thumb.

"It's over now," she said. "Just another day's work to you and why don't I get up and go. The Fremonts will have your letter saying their daughter died eight months ago in a hotel fire and was never identified. It's going to hurt them, but nothing could hurt them as much as the truth. Still you didn't have to twist things around this afternoon to save my skin. I can't help wondering about that, Paul."

"You can stop wondering about it," I said. "Maybe I believed all the hearts and flowers you gave me about being in love with your husband in spite of his money. Maybe I thought it was time Susan Griswold gave up trying to run you out of the house. Maybe I figured I had no right to prove to Lawrence Griswold that his angel had a brass halo. Or maybe I'm just another ham who couldn't pass up a chance to play God."

She didn't stay long after that. I continued to sit, smoking a cigarette and running a finger along the arm of my chair. I stood up finally and leaned against the window frame and looked down into Jackson Boulevard at the tiny figures of people hurrying along because everybody hurries these days.

"You and God," I said.

Howard Browne on Howard Browne

Born in Omaha, Nebraska. My mother was a school teacher, my father died four months before I was born. While residing in Lincoln, Nebraska, and after attending high school for three years, it seemed to me that attending school was interfering with my education. So I dropped out altogether.

In those days, for anyone my age, Lincoln offered few opportunities beyond jerking sodas or pumping gas. So, I hitchhiked to Chicago in search of a career. In turn, I was a shipping clerk, a waiter in a tuberculosis sanitarium, a wholesale produce salesman, an installer of Venetian blinds, a machine operator for a wood products plant, a department store skip-tracer, and credit supervisor for a chain of schlock furniture stores. Plus, somewhere along the line, a husband and the father of a son and daughter.

When all this was out of the way, I opted for a writing career.

My first effort was a pair of short stories aimed at the pulp magazine market. Ziff-Davis, a Chicago publisher, bought both stories for their new detective magazine and hired me as the editor. Eventually I became editor of their entire chain of pulps, and served as such till I lit out for Los Angeles to write for motion pictures and television. By that time I had to my credit eight novels and over two hundred stories for the magazines I edited.

Between 1956 and 1976, I wrote four major motion pictures, somewhere around 130 TV scripts, and served as story editor on various TV series. During those same years I went through a divorce, remarried and adopted a baby girl.

Now I'm back to writing novels, teaching screenwriting at the University of California, San Diego, and doing an occasional play-doctoring job on an ailing TV script.

Finding spare time has always been a problem for me.